THE GIRL
WHO CAPTURED
THE SUN

The Sheena Meyer Series

Book Three

JOA PRESS
FLORIDA

Books by L. B. Anne

CULY GIRL ADVENTURES SERIES (Ages 6-8)

Book One: Pickled Pudding

Book Two: Zuri the Great

Book Three (Coming Soon): Tangled

LOLO AND WINKLE SERIES (Ages 9-12)

Book One: Go Viral

Book Two: Zombie Apocalypse Club

Book Three: Frenemies

Book Four: Break London

Book Five: Middle School Misfit

THE SHEENA MEYER SERIES (Ages 12-14)

Book One: The Girl Who Looked Beyond the Stars

Book Two: The Girl Who Spoke to the Wind

Book Three: The Girl Who Captured the Sun

Middle School Group Guide

Here is a quick reminder of who's who in this middle school universe as described in book one.

The FPS (fips): the future pop stars—that's what *they* think anyway. They dance, they sing, they're popular, and God forbid they have a hair out of place at any time. They try to dress like the stars they're going to be without breaking the school dress code. Some don't care and will arrive in cropped tops and just deal with the consequences. As far as they're concerned, they're royalty and we are mere peasants.

The Unmentionables: They are mostly ignored, like they don't matter. But truthfully, they're cool. They're just introverts.

The Jokers: You know, like in Batman? They're playful and joke around a lot, which always gets them in trouble. They're harmless, but a little annoying at times. They fart a lot too. They'll make you sorry you ever inhaled.

The Sporties: Basketball, football, soccer—that's all they care about.

The Bookworms: They don't talk. They just sit and read.

The Troublemakers: Mean for no reason at all.

1

*J*ust a few months ago, I was a kid. Thirteen is not exactly a kid, but I feel I've aged a whole lifetime.

When you are a kid, things like vampires, creatures, and other worlds are scary but exciting. I used to watch all kinds of movies about legendary and otherworldly creatures. I read the books too—the ones my mom would allow (she polices everything). Those stories were fun because they were all fake. Then I turned thirteen and my world exploded. I found out monsters really do exist. How does that happen? Shouldn't we get a warning? That is not something you just spring on a person. But that's what happened to me. And, as unbelievable as my story seems, it's not over.

My story picks up right where we left off…

<hr />

As I walked through the front door of my house, a dark-haired man wearing a camel coat was leaving. He nodded toward us in passing.

"Daddy, who was that?"

"Mr. Tobias's son. His father added you to his will. Did you know that? He left this for you."

My mom and I glanced at each other as my dad handed me a large square package wrapped in brown paper.

I took the parcel back to the kitchen table and tore off the wrapping. It was an old leather-bound book about two inches thick and the size of a big photo album. You know, the kind your grandparents or great grandparents always have. On the cover was a brass symbol. Loops connected at the center of a circle, and symbols were inscribed around it.

My mom, anxious to see inside, stood so close to me I could feel her heartbeat on my arm. Or was it mine?

I opened the book and slammed it shut, shocked by what I'd seen.

"What is it?" she asked. "You couldn't have read anything that fast."

"His son told me they weren't able to read it," my dad said while heading for the back door.

The scent of barbequed meat drifted in as the door opened. Knowing my dad, he was trying to surprise me with my favorite turkey burgers with cheese on the inside that only he knew how to make.

I grabbed the book from the table and held it to my chest.

"What is it, Sheena?" my mom half-whispered.

"I-I don't know yet. I don't know if I'm ready to think about Mr. Tobias being gone. Every day, when I leave school, I can see his white house on Monroe Street. I imagine he's inside watching television and giving Nurse Paige a hard time. So in my head, he's still alive. Having something that belonged to him makes his passing real."

My mom exhaled as if she'd been holding her breath and rubbed my shoulders. "I can understand that. How about we light up the fire pit and sit out in the fresh air for a while before it gets too cold?"

I nodded, looking down at the floor. I couldn't make eye contact. Not yet. She would know I lied—well partially. How could I tell her I just saw my willow in that book?

"What would you like, warm apple cider or lemon tea?"

I wanted the apple cider because with it usually came mini powdered sugar donuts, but I chose the tea because my throat didn't quite feel back to normal yet after my almost drowning.

My mom sat in a chair in front of the steel fire pit, sipping ginger tea. I sat on a blanket under my willow tree, leaned back against it, and smiled while watching my dad flip burgers and joke with her. "Bee, I will burn yours until it's charcoal if you don't stop nagging me and let me do what I do."

My mom laughed and held up her smartphone. "Just keep talking. I'm recording how you threaten me so the world can see what you put me through."

Flames danced over the wood of the pit, and just above it, the air wavered from the heat, blurring the look of the chair on the other side of the pit. It made me think of the Murk. It wavered like that in the wind. I set my tea down and picked up the book that lay on the ground beside me, carefully placing it on my lap. My finger traced over the swirls of the symbol on the cover.

"Sheena, what's on your mind?" asked my dad, glancing over.

I shook my head. "Just thinking about how mysterious the world is."

My eyes met my mom's eyes. Hers had been wide, as if on alert.

"We think we know everything about everything, but we don't," I continued.

"Hmm...that's true."

My mom's eyes softened. I think she was unsure of what I might say. She relaxed and showed a hint of a smile.

"Jonas, watch what you're doing!" she exclaimed. She threw her blanket to the side, grabbed a jug from the table, and ran over to my dad.

Good. Their focus is off me.

I gently lifted the cover of the leather-bound book. It was so old, I thought it might creak like our stairs, or possibly fall apart. My eyes widened as I turned the pages. I sat forward. The entire book was written in the same symbols I'd seen in my dream—known only to angels, unreadable by humans.

But I understood them...

2

I thumbed through the book, looking up at my mom every few minutes. She kept glancing over at me, and frown lines formed on her forehead. I know she thought I didn't notice. Moms can't help but worry. She was concerned about what I may be experiencing or not telling her, I think. "No more secrets," she had said, and I promised. But when a book tells you that you can't share anything that's in it, do you? That means not even with your mom and dad, right?

My willow tree was sketched in the background of a page that told of a day when an angel would appear before children all over the world. One child would see an archangel. That child would be the last gleamer.

This is crazy, I thought as I closed the book. *This thing is telling of a special gleamer, and I'm that gleamer? I'm reading about myself?*

What's this? A handwritten note in the same symbols stuck out near the back of the book, like a sticky note. *It's from Mr. Tobias!*

I quickly stood. Some foolish part of me thought I could make it inside the house without my parents noticing and turning it into this huge deal. I mean, can't a girl go to the bathroom without a big announcement?

"Sheena, where are you going?" my mom asked as I stopped walking.

"Inside."

"Are you okay?"

"Just a little tired, and I'm cold."

My mom stood. "Let me help you."

There it is—huge deal. So predictable. "No, I'm okay. Seriously."

"Belinda, you know she doesn't like to be fussed over."

My mom shot my dad an irritated look. "Jonas, she just got out of the hospital. I don't care what she says, you know she's not one hundred percent yet. I will fuss as long as I—"

I thought I could make my exit as they argued. It was a good distraction, so I could get inside. But then, *Whoosh!*

My dad snuck up from behind me and picked me up, carrying me into the house. I giggled like a toddler. "Daddy, you shouldn't be picking me up."

"What Mama wants, Mama gets," he said over his shoulder. Which seemed to make my mom happy. "Where shall I take you, Madam?"

"Daddy, you are not carrying me up the stairs. You're still recovering from the car accident."

"Yes, I *am* carrying you upstairs. And don't worry about me, Baby Girl. I've had a miraculous recovery."

"Miraculous? You suddenly believe in miracles?"

"Hold on to your book, lassie," he said as he turned up the stairs and carried me without a moan or a grunt, like I weighed nothing. And I'm a whole ninety pounds.

"Wait, isn't that an old show about a dog. It is! Daddy, you called me a dog's name?"

"It means young girl, Sheena."

"I know. I was joking."

"Ha ha, funny," he replied and placed me on my bed.

I kissed him on the cheek before removing my arm from around his neck.

"Back to miracles," I said as I pulled my arms out of my coat.

"Oh boy."

"No, Daddy, listen. I think an angel was watching over you. You should really believe in angels."

"What makes you think I don't?"

"I thought—"

"I don't believe in spooky stuff: ghosts, goblins, monsters, and foolishness. But angels, they're real."

"So…" I hesitated and looked down at the goosebumps on my arm, not sure of what I wanted to say or how I was going to say it. "What if I told you…" I paused and looked around the room, expecting an angel to appear and stop me.

"Jonas!"

"What if you told me what?"

"Jonas!"

"What, Woman?"

"Ooh, Mom is going to get you for calling her that."

"I think your meat is burning!"

My dad shot out of the room, and I sat for a minute, waiting to hear his outburst when he opened the grill. No sounds of disappointment floated up to my window. He didn't even use the word he uses when something really goes wrong. It wasn't exactly a swear word, but it was as close as you could get to one in our house. And I sure wasn't allowed to say it.

Then I heard my mom's laughter, and I relaxed.

My dad believes. Since when?

I set Mr. Tobias's book on my bed, crossed my legs under me, and stared at it for a long time before opening it again to the handwritten message inside.

Don't be surprised you can read this, Little Gleamer.

I must've read that sentence ten times. A tear fell from my eye. Mr. Tobias always called me that.

> *The Lumen is written in the language of angels. If you are reading this, the Murk have accomplished what they've been trying to do for years. Don't worry, I was not afraid. It may have killed my flesh, but my soul lives on.*
>
> *This book holds the answers to many questions you have, including a list of instructions.*
>
> *Keep it safe, and it will keep you safe. It is the last that remains of the Gleamer Key. Study it and keep it in your heart. Do not lose hope, Little Gleamer. It is why you are who you are. I will see you again. I ask your forgiveness in not telling you everything sooner. I should have told you what you really were...*
>
> *May your vision be true.*

Wait, what? His words left me breathless and my head spinning. *What I really am? What does that mean? I'm a gleamer. That's what he told me. Nana agreed. What more could there be? Has Nana kept something else from me?* Those thoughts and more filled me as I lifted the book over my head and threw it across the room. It hit the wall under my window and fell to the floor.

With my eyes squeezed shut and fists balled, a yell escaped me that encompassed everything I'd been through—all the pain and deception. I screamed until my throat hurt.

Hugging my knees to my chest, I laid on my side and waited. How was I going to explain this? Any minute, my mom and dad would come charging in. But no one came. In fact, I could hear them talking over the fence to a neighbor.

A killer could be on the loose and trying to get me, and they wouldn't even know.

I dried my tears and sat up. Maybe I hadn't screamed as loud as I thought, thank goodness.

After a couple of deep breaths, I stood and walked over to the book. It lay open below my window, still intact.

Across the way, Dingy ran a toy car across his windowsill. Before I could stoop and pick up the book, he saw me and waved wildly to get my attention. *Sheesh, I'm looking right at you.*

I don't know why that kid was always so happy to see me. Dingy pointed at his car and rolled it over the windowpane. I gave him a thumbs-up just as his mom walked up behind him. While his attention was off me, I ducked out of view and picked up the book—*I guess I should call it by its name,* the Lumen—and looked it over. *No damage. I could probably throw it into a fire, and it wouldn't burn.*

"Sheena?"

I jumped and spun around. *How long had she been there?*

My mom looked concerned. I know she noticed I'd been crying, but she didn't mention it. "Dad fixed your plate."

"I'm not really hungry."

"Okay. I won't argue. I'll leave it in the oven for you." She studied me a moment and then closed the door behind her.

I stood there, staring at the door. *I should have told you what you really were...* echoed in my head.

"Mom!"

The door opened as if she'd still been standing on the other side waiting. "Yes?"

"Where's Daddy?"

"In the kitchen or out back. Why?"

"You know how you believed I saw something in the willow when I was little, but never told me you believed me?"

"Yes..."

"Is there anything else about me I don't know?"

"Like what?"

"Like gleamer stuff. Is there anything more?"

"I—"

She stopped just like that and turned to leave, then turned back and walked over to me. She lowered her voice. "You know what I know."

"But—"

She looked behind her and back at me. "Give Nana a call. Remember, the gleam skipped a generation. Nana is only allowed to tell me so much. But she will tell *you.*"

I still held the book. She tapped it. "Make sure you take care of that. I have the strangest feeling it's important."

"It's probably worth a ton of money," my dad said from behind her. "Come and eat this food, Baby Girl. You two have me down there slaving and then think you're not going to eat?"

"Okay, okay," I said, waving them out of my room. I wasn't hungry, but I'd say anything to get them off the subject of that book.

"You're hungry?"

"Famished."

My dad eyed me. "Famished, huh?"

"Yes, bring on the grub."

"Do you think you can part with that thing for a while?"

"Oops. I forgot I was holding it."

I backed up and put the Lumen on my bookshelf. I saw a flash of red out of the corner of my eye and looked toward the window. Dingy and his mom were crossing over the back yard with an aluminum foil covered container.

"Daddy, you invited people?"

"They smelled the grill," he yelled from the stairs.

I fell back onto my bed. *Now I'll never get some time alone to read.*

"Sheena!"

"Coming!"

3

*Y*ou would think it was summer and we were having a family barbeque. Different neighbors came in and out, leaving with plates of food. Really, Strong Street had to be the friendliest street in the world.

I sat at the kitchen table with my phone in my lap and threw my hand over the screen. I'd switched it to silent mode, but it kept lighting up with alerts. Five missed calls from Chana, three from Ariel, and one from Cameron. Two mentions on Instagram and several Snap alerts. Not a single call from Teddy.

"Dingy, what's your favorite thing about school?"

"People have birthdays, and their moms bring cupcakes," he said while dipping a potato wedge in onion dip and stuffing it in his mouth.

Everyone laughed. Then my dad started on one of his epic stories about his days in elementary school. His exaggerations were priceless. Like his walking twenty miles to school in Michigan's six-feet-of-snow winters, backward, uphill, with no shoes on while being chased by a bear—crazy stuff like that.

Dingy loved his stories. If I was Dingy's favorite person, my dad was definitely his second favorite. So while he was preoccupied, I excused myself, went into the butler's pantry, and dialed quickly.

"Hello," her voice sang rather than spoke. A warm feeling poured over me just from hearing her.

"Nana? Nana!"

"Sheena? Ha ha! Glory be, I was just thinking about you, Sweetie."

"Nana, look at your phone."

"Huh? Everyone at Bethel was praying for you. I'm so glad you're okay."

"Look at your phone, Nana."

"What? Why?"

"Nana—" I put my phone down at my side in exasperation.

"Nana, this is Facetime. This is not a phone call. It's visual. I can see your ear and headscarf."

"Sheena, where are you?" Dingy called from the next room.

"I'll be out in a minute." *I left him with a full plate of food. How is he done already?*

"Dingy, get back in here," his mom said. "We do not wander around other people's houses."

"I'm looking for Sheena."

"She'll be back."

"Nana, can you see me now?"

"Yes, I can, sweetie," her voice wisped with love. She wore a light blue terry cloth robe and a paisley headscarf.

"Hi."

"I know you didn't call me at this hour just to say hello."

I'd forgotten she goes to bed early. "Did I wake you?"

"No, I had a nap earlier. Sounds like you have company over."

"Neighbors."

"The hoity-toity ones?"

"Hoity-toity? I don't even know what that means," I said as I shook my head. "Nana, I called to find out if you left out anything—about being a gleamer. Maybe you forgot something?"

"Not that I can think of. Why?"

"Mr. Tobias said there's more."

"When?"

"Today. I mean, he left me a note in the Lumen."

Nana's eyes widened and she sat up. "Did you say the Lumen? Do you have the Lumen?"

"Yes, ma'am."

"Let me see it."

"It's upstairs. I can't get it right now."

"Describe it."

"It's brown leather and has a brass symbol on the cover."

"What does the symbol look like?"

"Loops that connect at the center of a circle."

"The symbol of angels…" her voice trailed off. "How did you get the Lumen, Sweetie?"

"Mr. Tobias left it to me in his will."

Nana looked away from the screen. "That means he knew he was going to die. I can't believe he had it all this time. That rascal."

"Nana, you knew him, didn't you? Why didn't you tell me?"

"There's a time and place for everything. We were old friends, bonded by the gleam."

"Bonded? What does that mean?"

"Sheena?" my mom said, walking into the pantry. She crossed her arms in front of her, thinking she'd caught me talking to friends during dinner. That was against the rules and could get my phone taken away.

"I'm talking to Nana," I mouthed to her.

"Oh, okay," she whispered and backed out. "She'll be right out," she told Dingy.

"Nana, I have to get back. What can you tell me? Is there anything else?"

"In the same way those loops connect on the cover, gleamers are connected, and protect each other."

I meant, was there anything else about me, and I think she knew it. "What's the circle in the center?"

"The sun."

"Nana, am I something more than I know I am?"

"Of course, you are."

My heart rate increased. There was no way to prepare myself for what she was going to tell me. I backed up against the pantry's cabinet doors. At least if I fainted, maybe I'd just slide down to the floor.

"Tobias was the strongest gleamer there was. He's passed on everything he knew to you. Now you're the strongest."

"Why? Because I have that book? That means what?"

Nana continued as if she didn't hear me. "And the last. No matter what Tobias was trying to tell you, there is nothing you need to be afraid of. Remember, we are on the side of all that is good, all that is pure, and all that is holy. Give it time. All the answers to every question you have will come."

"Skidamarink-a-dingy-dingy," Dingy sang as he ran into the pantry with his red cape flowing behind him.

"Shh..."

"Who's that?"

"That's Dingy. I've gotta go, Nana. Love you, bye," I said quickly and ended the call.

Dingy lifted his head toward my phone, "Bye, Nana."
He grabbed my hand. "Come out of here."

I followed him back into the kitchen. *If only I could bottle up all that happiness and innocence*, I thought as I watched Dingy prance around. I realized I never wanted him to lose that. I never wanted him to find out about real monsters—any more than he already had. How could I protect him from that? And from the nightmares? Who would protect me from mine?

4

*D*ear God, please don't let me have a bad dream...
That was my request every night since coming home from the hospital. After I said my prayers, I pulled my curls up into a ponytail, sat back against my pillows, and ran my fingers over the symbol on the cover of the Lumen. It was the symbol of angels, just like Nana said. I looked it up. Who knew there was such a thing?

I then pushed the book under my pillows and laid back, hugging my fuzzy pillow. *No nightmares tonight,* I told myself. I believed. I mean, I really believed that night was going to be a good night. After all, I knew that after you prayed, you had to fully believe you would receive what you prayed for.

Three hours later, my body jerked forward as I awoke with a scream stifled in my throat. My bedroom was dark, except for the thin strip of light shining in from the hall. The door was barely cracked open, even though I'd insisted my parents never close it when I slept, at all.

I looked around my room in a panic. My next steps were crucial, and I had them down to a science. To keep from getting captured by the boogie man you must throw your feet over the side of the bed as fast as you can and find your slippers. (The floor is freezing this time of the year, and you may have to run clear out the front door.) Then get out of the room as fast as possible, so whatever was in your dream can't get you.

Only for me it didn't stop there. I did what I'd been doing most nights lately—tiptoed down the hall and looked up at the entrance to the attic, which looked like a passage to a tomb of ghosts, vampires, and whatever could scare the living daylights out of me at that time of night. I walked along the wall, not turning my back to it, so a creature couldn't pop out and drag me away.

At the end of the hall, I entered my parents' bedroom. The sound of a gentle waterfall over string instruments played softly. My mom said it helped her sleep. And I believed it because their room had a different feeling than mine. It was full of love and warmth, and calm.

From the foot of the bed, I climbed into their king-sized bed. Right between them. My dad, in a restful sleep, grunted and made room for me.

I finally exhaled as I laid my head back on my mom's pillow, feeling her light breaths at the side of my face. I was safe now. Safe from that feeling in my room. Safe from my worst imagination of what might be in the attic at night. Safe from my dream.

Where is my angel? It's all his fault. He left me. He said he had to go. An archangel can't just up and leave someone like that. Can he? Can it? This is not at all good for my emotional development.

I shivered, remembering my dream. If darkness had a feeling, that is what it would feel like. Fear, pain, sorrow—the Murk.

I awoke feeling something heavy over my mouth. My mom's arm stretched over my face. Maybe she was trying to make me feel protected while I slept, and her arm moved from across my stomach to my head somehow. But her arm was dead weight over my nose and mouth, cutting off my air supply. How did she have the nerve to say *I* was a crazy sleeper?

My mom felt me moving and turned over. I scooted off the bed, stood, and stretched. My first day back to school after the accident. *Am I ready? I'd better be because I have a lot of catching up to do.* I just didn't want anyone fawning over me.

Ooh… Butter and vanilla. The pleasant smell hit me and made me rush to shower and dress. By the time I got to the kitchen, my mom was there. I guess my dad's pancakes brought her downstairs too.

"Good morning, Bed Invader. Are you ready to get back to normal life, Baby Girl?"

Ha! Bed Invader. That's a good one. That's my alter ego. "Daddy, watch it! The sleeve of your robe dipped in the batter."

"Oops. Clothing fibers and sloughed-off skin cells should make it real tasty."

"Ha! That doesn't scare me. I'm eating them anyway. And when did I not live a normal life?" I asked as I pushed a fork through three pancakes and placed them on my plate. "Isn't this a normal life?" All the while I was thinking, *Dad, you have no idea how abnormal my life is.*

"You know what I mean. Going back to school."

My mom set her glass of orange juice down and stood behind me, messing with my hair. "She doesn't have a choice in that. She's going back even if I have to drag her."

I ducked and tilted my head to the side, away from her. "Mom, my hair is fine."

"No, it's not. Separate the curls more."

"You guys are acting like this is the first day of school or something. Plus, it's a Friday. Why couldn't I just start back on Monday? You know you're going to miss me."

My mom bumped me with her hip. "Miss you? I hardly saw you. You spent the majority of the time with your nose in that book Mr. Tobias left you. You can't even read it."

I bumped her back. "That doesn't make it any less interesting. I'm determined to figure it out."

My dad hugged me from the side, turned, and flipped a pancake. "You will, Baby Girl."

"Mom is sleeping on my skills," I said through a mouth full of food.

"Speaking of sleeping—"

I gulped down my orange juice and grabbed my pre-packed lunch from the fridge. "Hold that thought, Daddy. My ride's here."

My mom looked out of the window. "How did you know that?"

"I heard the horn."

"What horn?"

Chana's dad beeped twice. "*That* horn."

I kissed my dad on the cheek, dipped my finger in syrup, smeared it over my lips, and ran along the island to my mom. She tried to duck, but I was too fast. I blew a syrup zerbert on her cheek.

"Yuck, Sheena. Oh my gosh. I can't believe you did that."

I ran to the foyer, laughing as she swung at my bottom.

"See that? You. You created that," I heard her telling my dad.

5

*C*hana opened the rear door of the car for me and I jumped in quickly.

"Hey, Sheena."

"Good morning, I. D. Thanks for the ride." I. D. stood for Interim Dad. I'd either call him I-Daddy, I-Dad, or shorten it to I. D. He always laughed when I called him that. But he really did act like my father when my own dad wasn't around.

"No worries. *We're* glad you're back."

"Dad, stop."

"*Someone*—and I'm not going to name any names— was a mess without you."

I turned to Chana, waiting for her comeback.

She knew what I was thinking. "I've got nothing. When you're on thin ice and grounded for life, there's not much you can say."

Her dad's reflection in the rearview mirror smiled in response, and I laughed. "Poor thing."

"You're all chipper today," Chana accused.

"My dad cooked."

"Wow, and you didn't bring out any for us?"

"Oops, my bad. Count it to my head and not my heart. I got you next time, I. D."

Chana and I didn't talk much the rest of the way to school. We never did, around parents. But as soon as we were free—and that could take forever because of how slow the student drop-off line was—and walked the thirty-three brisk steps from the car into the building, we were motor-mouths.

Chana pulled me along by the sleeve, as if I didn't know where I was going. "I really am *extremely* glad you're back." She emphasized extremely. "What is hot chocolate without marshmallows?"

I laughed. "Peanut butter without bacon..."

"Seriously? Is that the best you could do? Gross. Anywho, just so you know, the pack has lots of questions. I didn't tell them anything, though."

"As in a pack of wolves? What pack?"

Chana walked backward, in front of me, blocking my view, without a care for who she bumped into. "Our cohorts. Our posse. Cameron and Bradly."

"Wow, really?"

"The team, okay? Is that better? It's just an easy way of saying the people who worked with us on you-know-what. You know, the three who were in the shed with us when that thing happened? *That* team." She glanced behind her. "Ta-dah!" she said as she held her hands out as if she were presenting my locker to me for the first time.

"What in the name of arts and crafts did you people do?" The top portion of my locker was covered in colorful paper flowers with buttons at the centers. The rest was covered in notes, pictures, and cards. "It looks like a shrine!"

"Hey, I didn't have anything to do with it. Just smile like you love it," she whispered. "Now gush like you appreciate it so much."

I was bad at it. Gushing wasn't really part of my personality.

At least the notes and flowers were taped on and not glued, so I could easily remove them. There were some really nice messages from students and teachers, and a few weird ones from the jokers—meant to make me laugh, I guess.

Chana looked over my hair and outfit as I put my coat in my locker. It's not like I wore anything special. Jeans, t-shirt, zip up fleece sweater—my usual.

I placed my hand on my hip. "Do I have your approval, Mom? Am I on fleek?"

"Please stop. You are no good with slang," she said with a laugh. "Plus, no one says that anymore, I keep telling you."

"What about 'slammin?' Do they still say that?" I joked.

"I love you, but I *will* duct tape your mouth."

I glanced behind me. "People are staring."

Chana frowned and looked over my shoulder. "Who?"

"What are you going to do, punch them?"

"Yeah, each and every one of them. I'm going to run down the hall socking people in the jaw. You get a broken jaw. And you get a broken jaw!" she yelled as she pointed at kids in the hall.

"Why are you threatening people?" I laughed. "That is so not cool."

"Just ignore them.

"Ooh, that's the warning bell. Sorry to have to cut the convo short, She-she. I can't be late for class anymore. See you later, She-bear."

"She-bear? Okay."

We did our bestie gesture—bumped fists, crossed arms in the air, and brought them down. Chana quickly disappeared into a sea of coats and backpacks, and I turned down the hall toward my class.

There were plenty of whispers, giggles, finger-pointing, and odd looks. I expected it. Even though these were the same kids that were on the news making a big deal about me almost drowning and acted like they were all in such turmoil, they sure weren't racing toward me in tears, hugging me, telling me they were glad I was alive or happy to see me. Except for the See You at the Pole kids. The way they crowded around me; I might as well have been the flagpole they would usually gather around to pray. "Thanks, guys," I said as I pushed through the group—a few in the back just nosey students who wanted to hear what might be said.

"There's the hero," one of the FPS sneered as I passed.

"She is, so be quiet," said Bradly.

I am not the kind of person that needs someone to defend them, but it was nice to hear Bradly come to my defense after we'd been enemies for so long.

A hand reached up over the heads in the hall and waved at me. She squeezed through the students. A huge grin covered her face.

"Sheena, you're back," she exclaimed as she smacked into me with a hug.

Oof!

I laughed. "You about knocked the air out of me, Ariel."

"Sorry, I'm a little excited to see you. Do you feel okay? Do you need anything?"

"Ariel, Ariel, stop fussing over me. I'm fine." Her eyes were as bright as ever. I don't think anything could dim that shine.

"Are you sure?"

"Yes."

"What about you? Is everything okay?"

"Excellent."

"I'm glad. How is your—"

"You dropped something," she said of a folded note on the floor.

"Oh, it probably fell out of my book. There were so many get well notes stuffed in my locker, one might have gotten stuck. I'll have to take them all home and read them later."

"I'll help you if you want. I have to stop at the office before class. I'll see you later, Sheena."

"Okay, I—" *Yep, just walk away while I'm talking to you like always. I guess some things never change.*

I unfolded the note as I walked.

Author Stephen Woodruff

I thought it an odd thing to put in my locker. Maybe my English teacher wanted me to check him out. Maybe he wrote about drowning or something. I put the note in my pocket.

Ariel watched me from the end of the hall and waved. As I raised my arm to return the gesture, a kid came out of nowhere and bumped past me, shoving me into another student. "Sorry," I told her and stooped to pick up the book she'd dropped. "I guess I was in his way.

"Excuse me, would have sufficed!" I yelled after him. The tall, dark-haired boy kept walking down the hall. I only saw the back of him, but something about him was familiar.

6

*I*t was more of the same between each period. Some students saying hello, others whispering, and some smiling in my direction. There were a few eye rolls too.

"Welcome back," someone said as I walked into the cafeteria with my sack lunch. "Hungry, are we?" asked one of the boys of the joker group because of the size of my bag.

"Shh... stop it," someone whispered. I guess it was too soon to make fun of the girl who almost died.

The bookworms didn't even notice me. They were engrossed in conversation. Yes, the bookworms that did nothing but read during lunch were actually talking. And they were excited. Jasmine held a book and mentioned the media center. My ears perked up hearing the name Woodruff. *Maybe one of them left me the note.*

I backed up to their table. "I wasn't trying to listen in on your conversation, but did you just say, Woodruff."

"Yes, Stephen Woodruff. Why, do you know of him?" asked Jasmine. Her messy blonde bun fell over to the side as she spoke.

"Of course, he's an author."

They looked surprised, and at the same time, happy to have another person in their world.

"I'm so excited he's coming to Nelson," said Rebecca. "Aren't you?"

"Uh, yeah."

"I'm like freaking out. Which book is your favorite?" asked another girl, Melissa, who for once was not chewing on her hair.

"You have to be more specific, Lis" said Rebecca. "He has too many books. What about his latest series?"

"My favorite is book three. You know, *When Darkness Returns?*" said Jasmine.

"Oh yeah, darkness… Uh-huh."

"Did you resonate with any of the characters?" asked Melissa.

"I did," said another girl, pushing her glasses up on her nose. And all I'm thinking is, *if I can see all the smudges on your lenses, I know you can. Please, clean them!*

I could not believe how excited they were to discuss this. Melissa bounced up next to me, started to touch me, but pulled back. "Cassie. I really understood her. I think the darkness represented her inner struggle as a teen."

"No, I kind of felt like there was a spiritual aspect," said Rebecca. "What about you?"

"Well, I—"

"Do you want to join our book club?"

"Me?"

"Sheena!"

Saved.

"Gotta go. I'll talk to you guys later."

I rushed over to Chana and held on to the arm of her denim jacket, allowing her to lead me away from the bookworm lunch table. Any direction would do. Whatever it took to keep those bookworms from learning I was a fraud and knew nothing about Stephen Woodruff or his novel. "Thank you, thank you, thank you."

"Why are you so relieved?"

"I didn't know how to get away from them."

"Do not let me catch you at that table again."

"They're not so bad."

"Maybe not, but we don't identify with any one group, remember? Therefore, we do not sit with the different groups in here. However, they may join *us* if they like. As you say, 'We're the *crème de la crème.*'"

"To be honest, it's just the two of us. Is that really a group?"

"No, there's more. We have Theodore and your buddy—happy girl—Ariel. That makes four and that's a group. Where is the little cherubim, anyway?"

"I don't know."

As soon as we sat down, Bradly and Cameron left their groups and sat at our table.

"Well? Where is it?" asked Cameron.

"What?"

"The book."

I glared at Chana. "Really?"

"It kind of slipped out."

"I'm not bringing it here."

"Chana said his son brought it to your house?" Cameron asked while stuffing a potato chip in his mouth.

"Yes. He left it to me in his will."

Bradly sat braiding her waist-length braids into sections. "Why would angels need a book? They have the Bible."

"The Bible is for us, human flesh," Cameron said while trying to pinch Bradly as she squirmed away.

"Don't even think about it," Chana said as he reached toward her.

Cameron pulled back from her. "That book is like history or instructions for people like Sheena. Am I right?"

"How did you know that?"

"It's common sense."

Bradly tossed her braid over her shoulder, leaned forward, and placed her palms flat on the table. "What I want to know is if it's over. Can we rest easy now? Well, not just us." She waved her hand around the room. "Everybody. Are we safe? Does the book have information like that?"

Chana gave me a look that I knew meant not to say anything.

"Well?"

They acted like I could share absolutely all information with them because we were some kind of monster slaying team or something. But I read that I couldn't talk about what was in the Lumen. I didn't really know the answer to Bradly's question anyway.

They watched me like they were starving, and I had the next morsel of food they'd been waiting on. So I said what I thought Nana would say. "Only time will tell."

Cameron pointed. "Don't even try it. That's avoidance. Come on, tell."

"No, it's not."

"Can she eat in peace without you badgering her, Cameroon?"

"Do better. Is that supposed to be funny that you called me a country? Can you try to act thirteen? Name calling is so four years ago."

"Whatever."

"Whatever," Cameron repeated, mimicking Chana's voice. He turned back to me. "It's your fault. You made us believe in stuff we didn't even believe in—stuff we didn't even know existed. Now you want to leave us hanging? You don't have to tell us everything. Just give us a little something." He held his thumb and index finger with a small space between them. "Just a teeny tiny bit of information."

"Okay, okay. Let me ask you something…" I looked around, making sure no one was listening, and lowered my voice.

"What if I told you I know what happens when you die?"

Chana spun toward me as if I had snatched food from her tray. Cameron and Bradly moved in closer.

"Really?"

"Are you being serious?" He didn't even notice the potato chips that dropped in his lap. They were all in. I could have told them just about anything, and they would've believed it.

I twisted off the cap of my juice and took a big swig of it.

Cameron backed up. "She's stalling, she doesn't know."

"Do you? Do you know?" asked Bradly. "Is that what happened to you when you drowned—"

"Almost drowned. She's still here."

"Do you want to know or not?"

They nodded.

I lowered my voice again, and Cameron moved back in toward us. "It's so quiet and then there's this beautiful music. And it's dark at first, but not like scary-dark. As if nothing else exists—"

"Ahem!"

We all jumped. A big bear of a middle-schooler-man loomed over us.

Cameron held his chest. "Sheesh man, are you trying to give someone a heart attack? You are too big to just appear like that."

"Hey, Justin." I handed him a sack from inside my bag. "Lunch and dessert, right? Just like we agreed. I didn't forget."

"I wasn't going to hold you to it, but thanks. I just came over to ask you what's up with Theodore."

"What about him?"

"Heyyyyy! Is it a party over here, or what?" Teddy joked as he approached and placed his arm around Justin.

He seemed like the same old good-natured Teddy to me. I glanced at Chana and she shrugged.

"What are we talking about?" asked Teddy. "What did I miss?"

"We're talking about Justin eating a whole refrigerator for lunch," said Cameron.

Justin took a seat at our table. "You know you want some."

"That's right. I do."

Justin snatched the bag away from Cameron's hand.

"See, our group is growing," Chana whispered.

"Let me see what you've got," said Teddy. He looked in the bag and made a face at Cameron because Justin allowed him to look and not Cameron. "Why does he get a sub?"

"It's a long story," I replied.

"Because I helped her sneak out of school."

"Ooh!"

"Justin!"

"You didn't say it was a secret."

7

I didn't get a hello, welcome back, or anything from Teddy, and the first thing he had to say to me was 'why does he get a sub?' No. I don't think so. I stood and pushed Teddy away from the group. "See what else is in her bag," I heard Cameron say. I didn't have to turn around to know Chana had snatched the bag from him.

"Owww!" he exclaimed.

"Where have you been today, Teddy? Why are you avoiding me?"

"What are you talking about? I've been at school. I'm right here."

"You haven't returned my calls. I texted you that I was coming back today. You didn't respond."

"You did?"

"You know I did. You didn't even act surprised to see me just now. And what is going on with your hair. When was the last time you went to the barber? I know you are not letting your hair grow for dreads again, because if you were you would have told me. We're friends, and that's what friends do, right?" I hoped I was making my point.

Teddy looked everywhere but at me and opened his mouth to speak, but I cut him off.

I shook my head. "I don't know what's going on with you, but you're acting really weird, and I don't do part-time friendships. My house. This evening. And don't make any excuses."

"Well, *you're* still as bossy as ever."

I looked past him at the tall man walking toward us, wearing a suit. My frown flipped to a smile.

"Sheena, welcome back," said Principal Vernon.

I gave Teddy a *I'm serious about what I said* look as he approached us.

"Looking sharp, Mr. V."

"Jason, get off that table," he said as he pointed and then turned back to me.

"You had us all worried.

"Dwayne, walk it to the trash bin, don't throw it," he yelled at a boy near the back wall. "I'm glad you're back." He patted my shoulder as he stepped past me. "If you need anything at all, you know where to find me."

"Yes, sir." I wondered if he'd patted my shoulder to keep from shaking my hand, in case I could see something he didn't want me to see. Not that I could still do that.

I turned back to continue fussing at Teddy, but he'd gone back to the lunch table.

"I-I do need something..."

Principal Vernon turned back.

"I need permission to interview the author that's visiting—for the school newsletter."

Principal Vernon looked relieved. "Already back to work. Good for you. That's easy. I thought it was going to be something like— Never mind. Pick up your pass from the office after lunch."

"Thank you."

Chana ran up to me. "I saw you talking to Mr. V. What was that about?"

"Oh, nothing."

"Don't start that. Remember, we don't let you do things alone."

I stared at her for a moment.

"What?"

"That's what Teddy says—used to say." I guess he didn't care anymore. Maybe the gleamer stuff was too much for him. Maybe it would run off everyone I cared about.

Chana snapped her fingers in my face. "Stop that. Get out of your head. You think too much. Are we still meeting up tonight?"

"Yep."

"*Na Na Na-na*," I sang as I rocked my head back and forth and twirled in a circle with my headphones on, dancing to my favorite Stevie song. Stevie was always there when I needed her. Stevie Nicks, that is.

My friends laugh at my music choices. It is not my fault my mind developed a special appreciation for the classics at an impressionable age. It just shows how, ummm… Eccentric! Yeah, that's a good word for me. My taste in music shows how eccentric I am.

I hopped up onto the window seat and back down before my dad could yell, "Sheena, if you don't get your butt down from there!"

Of course, I would obey, but he was all talk now. At least for a while, until the shock of me almost drowning wore off. I mean, would you really threaten your daughter that almost died just two weeks before? With any luck, I could use that accident for a good six months to get me out of trouble.

I stopped spinning around and reached for the window frame, steadying myself. It had snowed the night before, and again while I was in school. The backyard looked like a winter scene from a stock photo or a Christmas card. I was glad for the snow. With everything so white, it made it easier to spot something dark, like the Murk. Not that I'd seen any sign of the Murk.

Lana's branches were iced over and covered in snow. When I was four years old, I thought the branches of my willow tree resembled hair, so I named her. An only child must have a friend to play with, right? Lana was mine. I ran in circles around that tree while dragging my toy dog on a leash.

Hmmm... a dog. Maybe we should get a dog. I bet a dog would alert us if something evil was around. And it could sleep in my room.

I looked at Lana as if she were a person and it was my first time meeting her. *Oh, you're an angel? I'm Sheena Meyer, Gleamer. Nice to meet you.* I smiled to myself. For the first time in weeks, I was simply being a kid. Well, thirteen is not exactly a kid. I don't know why I kept forgetting I was a teen. It was still pretty new to me and hadn't set in, I guess.

I bobbed my head to the beat of the music pounding in my ears. From the corner of my eye, I saw movement. High up on the wall. My heart jumped in my chest as I slowly turned my head.

"Daddy!" I screamed.

It froze like it knew I'd seen it, although it wasn't facing me.

Why wasn't he coming to my rescue? "Daddy!"

My headphones pulled away from my ear and I jumped so high I probably almost touched the ceiling. My dad held the left earpad away from my ear.

I grasped my chest. "You scared me."

"Turn those down. Why were you calling me like something was happening down here?"

I pointed. "Look."

"Oh boy."

"Yep. We have mice."

The critter held on for dear life at the top of the drapes.

"Daddy, I can't live in a house with mice. What are we—"

"Shh...before your mom hears. She'll want to burn down the house."

"How did it get in here?"

"It's winter. They're seeking shelter."

"They?"

"If there is one, there's more. I'll have to inspect the house and find out how they're getting in. Not a word of this to your mom. We'll set traps tonight."

"Sheena!" my mom called from upstairs.

"Yes, ma'am."

"Bring me the sweater that's hanging in the laundry room, will you?"

"Okay!" I stopped walking. *Wait, did he just say we?*

8

"Got it! Mom, I need to ask you something," I yelled as I ran up the stairs and entered my parents' bedroom. I mean, the worst she could say was no, right? She might even think it was a good idea. My dad would be okay with it, I already knew. It was my mom I'd have to convince, and there was no greater debater than me.

You've got this, Sheena. Walk right in there and demand a dog. No, don't demand. Just ask her for one and then ask her to think about it. Yeah, that's the best approach. Tell her you'll do everything. They won't have to lift a finger to help take care of it.

"What can I help you with, my dear?"

"Mom, please put some clothes on!"

"I do have clothes on. I'm in my thermals and I'm getting dressed," she said as she pulled on her jeans.

"Just put some clothes on, please. I have company coming."

"What are you trying to say? I don't look good?"

She lifted her thermal shirt and grabbed her belly. "Look at all of this. This is you in twenty years or so."

I covered my eyes with one hand while trying to find the wall with the other. "Mom, no. My eyes! I'm blinded!"

"And this is the scar from where the doctor had to do an emergency c-section to deliver you."

"Yes, I know the story."

"I was in labor for nineteen hours—" we said at the same time.

"Oh, I guess you *do* know the story. But look at it."

"I've seen it."

"You have?"

"Mom, stop playing. You walk around naked in front of me all the time."

"That's because we're both girls. Women do that."

"What's going on up there?" my dad yelled from the stairs.

"Mom, please." I looked out of the window, hearing a car door slam. A hooded white furry coat ran up to the front porch. The doorbell rang and the front door opened.

"See, she's here."

"I can do what I want to do in my own house. And what I would like to do is not awake shivering, finding your almost-grown-body in my bed with my comforter tucked around you, Mrs. I'm-not-afraid-if-you-encounter-a-creature-talk-to-it-or-it's-a-missed-opportunity. Or whatever you said."

I acted like I hadn't heard a word. Besides, I was just a kid back then when I said all of that. Now I'm a few months older.

"Daddy, make Mom put some clothes on!"

My mom pulled her sweater over her head as he entered the room.

"It's called respect, Sheena. That body right there nursed you for two years."

"*Blech!* Please stop grossing me out."

"That was a crazy day, now that I think about it," my mom mumbled to herself, thinking about the delivery. "Just everything that happened that led up to the c-section..."

I backed up, watching her think aloud, as she walked toward her ensuite.

"Like something was trying to—"

"Leaving now."

"I forgot about the fall. But what caused—wait, Sheena. What did you want to ask me?"

"Never mind." I ran down the stairs. "Hey, girl!"

"You guys are so funny," Chana said while removing her wet boots. She pulled a pair of fuzzy rubber bottomed socks out of her bag and put them on.

I rolled my eyes. "Yeah, we're just hilarious. Come on downstairs. Teddy should be here soon. How were the roads?"

"A sheet of ice. We slid at an angle like five times. My mom threatened to turn around. I don't know why she didn't just let me walk."

"Yeah, you could've worn ice skates."

"We've walked in worse weather than this."

"Keyword, we. If a car slid across the street, at least I could push you out of the way."

I sat on the sofa and watched Chana remove one of her layers of sweaters. Two long braids hung in front of her face, and the rest of her hair was pulled up into a curly ponytail. Her nose was pink from the cold.

"You guys don't have heat in your car?"

"We do, but we live too close for it to warm up good."

Chana looked…human—like any other African American teenager. I mean she didn't glow or anything. She'd revealed, or rather I'd figured out, what she was. So when we were alone, I guess I expected her to transfigure or something. What would that even look like?

"I haven't told my parents or Nana about you, by the way."

"Told them what?"

"Who you are."

She looked at me strangely.

"Really, Chana?"

48

"I keep telling you I have no idea what you're talking about."

I stared at her with my lips pursed. "Yeah. Okay."

In front of the sofa, was an ottoman that served as a coffee table. Chana reached across it and studied the notepad I left there. "What's this?"

"Notes. Stop trying to change the subject."

"No. Really. Notes on what?"

I stared at her with my lips pursed and sighed hard to show my frustration. "Mrs. Pierce's class is going to the media center tomorrow. An author is visiting. I heard the bookworms mention it at lunch."

"Oh, when I called you from their table?"

"Yes. They were really excited, so I knew something big was happening. I asked that girl, Jasmine, about the book she was reading, and although I'm not part of the reading rainbow group—"

"Stop hating."

"I'm not—they shared everything. He's going to discuss being an author, which I'm interested in…"

"Then what's that funky look for? You don't like his books?"

"I looked him up. Check this out." I showed her Stephen Woodruff's website on my laptop.

"There's a lot of books here."

I pointed. "Yes, but look at that one."

"Okay…"

"No. Read the description."

"Whoa, is he talking about—that sounds like the Murk."

"That's what *I* said."

She jumped up, excited. "We have to question him. We have to get in there."

"I'm already on it. I got permission from Mr. V to attend the visit for the school newsletter."

"Good idea. We need to read that book, too."

"I've already downloaded it. We've got a lot of reading to do tonight."

"What do you mean we?"

I stood, hearing the doorbell. "Teddy's here."

Chana didn't say anything. She usually cracked a joke as soon as I mentioned his name. "Are you okay?"

She turned and rested her elbows on the back of the sofa. "It's just all of these things happening. Everything seems to be connected. Nothing is coincidental anymore. I mean, think about it. Seeing that angel, meeting Mr. Tobias, Nana—just everything. Now an author is coming to the school and he's written about the Murk?"

"Then there's the note."

"What note?"

"That someone stuck in my locker with the author's name on it."

Chana's eyes widened. "Who put it there? And why?"

"I don't know."

"See, it's like a bunch of pieces of a puzzle that fit together."

"That, or you're getting a little spooky." I laughed it off, but she was right.

"Ha ha. Whatever. Just bring Mr. Tobias's book down with you."

9

"It's freezing out there," said Teddy as he removed his coat, blew into his hands, and rubbed them together.

I'd never seen him look so drawn. Was he ill? "You look tired. Did you walk?"

"Yep."

"Why?"

"No ride."

"It's not like this was an emergency, Teddy. You could've gotten a ride with Chana or stayed home."

"No, I couldn't. You would've gotten all mad—" He looked over at the bouquet of flowers on the hall table. "Someone sent you those?"

"I got tons of flowers and plants." I pointed into the living room and dining room. "We have them all over the house. You would think there was a funeral."

"Cameron and Family."

I looked back. Teddy placed the card back inside the stick holder.

"Uh, yeah. Chana's waiting downstairs. You can head down. I'll be right there."

"Sheena, wait."

"What's up?"

"I'm sorry I didn't come to see you sooner."

"I wasn't in the hospital that long—"

"But I could've come by to check on you or to see if you needed anything."

"Teddy, it's okay. Your mom came by."

"She did?"

"You don't know that your mom came by?"

"Oh, yeah, yeah. I forgot."

That didn't sound right at all. "Teddy, what—"

"Theodore," Chana yelled up the stairs.

Teddy looked down into the basement.

"Well, it's about time. Get down here with your big-headed self."

He brought the side of his flat hand to his neck. "Just like this. See this? A karate chop straight to the throat. That's what you've got coming," he told her.

I laughed. "I'll be right down with snacks."

"When did you get so hospitable?"

Teddy, Chana, and I sat on the floor around Mr. Tobias'
leather-bound book, staring at it. Teddy glanced at me.
"This is it, huh?"

I nodded.

He held onto the toes of his socked feet, trying to warm
them. "Well, are we just going to sit here all evening
looking at it, or are you going to open it?"

Chana nudged me. "Why are you acting so spooky about
it?"

"Because of what's in it."

"Let me guess, the book floated and glowed with
lightning shooting out of it and opened itself up to a page
about you. And if that happened, you better have filmed it,
so it can go viral online."

"I know, right? People would argue in the comments
about whether it's real or not—"

"We'd be famous."

"We? Wait, why are you guys acting like that could
actually happen? That only happens in novels about witches
and stuff, and movies. This is real life stuff. Spiritual
warfare."

"So what's in it?"

I lowered my voice. "I can't interpret all of it. But it tells
of things that have happened and are going to happen."

"What kind of things?"

"In the spirit realm."

"But?"

"But what?"

"What else? I can tell there's something more."

"I'm in it." I said, careful to not give any details.

"You're in spiritual warfare?"

I tapped on the cover. "No. I'm in this book."

Chana and Teddy looked at each other and then burst with laughter.

"You need to stop it."

"I don't believe it. Show us."

Teddy lifted a corner of the page and pulled his hand back with a start. The edge burned as if someone held a match to it. We shielded ourselves, throwing our arms up in front of us as flames shot up halfway to the ceiling. "Oh my gosh..."

Chana threw her orange pop over it. "What did you do?"

Teddy placed his fingers in his mouth. "Nothing. I just touched it, and that thing burned me."

"How can a book burn you?"

"You just saw what happened. Maybe no one else is supposed to touch it."

"My parents did. Mr. Tobias' son did."

Chana turned toward the stairs. "Wait. Did you guys hear something?"

Teddy leaned in over the page. "Whoa, the burn is gone. That's crazy. It's like some kind of ancient writing. But the leather of the cover is nowhere near that old. So what does it say?"

"It tells of a re—"

Chana grabbed my arm. "You said you weren't allowed to tell us what it says. I mean, look what just happened to Theodore for touching it."

I started to speak, but Chana held a finger to her lips and looked behind her. My dad stood on the steps.

"What's going on, guys? Is something burning down here?"

Any smoke or evidence of the flame was gone.

"Nope. What's going on with you, Papa Bear?" Chana asked as she used her foot to slide the book under the couch. "Are you trying to show off how good your leg is working again?"

My dad laughed. "It is definitely good to get around like I used to. What's up, Theodore?"

He stood. "Hey, Mr. Meyer."

My dad walked over to us and looked at Teddy strangely. "Is everything okay with you, Theodore?"

"Yes, sir."

"Everything's fine at home?"

"Yes, sir."

"Daddy, what's with all the questions?"

"Nothing. I just haven't seen or talked to Theodore in a while." He talked to me, but he didn't take his eyes off Teddy. He studied him. "If you ever need to talk, I'm here." He paused for a moment, as if waiting for something.

"Earth to Dad—"

"I'll leave you guys to your secret meeting or whatever you're doing," he replied and headed back upstairs.

"What was that about?" Chana and I both looked at Teddy.

He ignored us and walked away.

"Where are you going?"

"To turn the heat up."

"Ah, ah, ah," said my dad from the top of the stairs. "He who pays the bills controls the furnace."

"Do you think your dad heard us?"

"He didn't act like it. And you know he doesn't believe in this kind of stuff. He definitely would've said something."

"Bring the book back out."

"No. Leave it there for now. Grab those napkins and some hand soap from the bathroom. We need to clean up this sticky mess."

"I'll get it. You fill Theodore in about the author visit."

He looked back and forth at us. "What author visit? And why would I want to know about it?"

"Oh, you don't want to know? What happened to all of that 'stop shutting me out' stuff?"

"Who cares about an author?"

"Okay, video game it is," I replied as I threw the wet napkins in the trash. *Fine*, I said to myself. If Teddy could act like he didn't want to know, I could act like not telling him was fine with me.

Chana shook her head. "You guys are such children."

"That's definitely why we live with our parents," Teddy quipped.

We spent the rest of the evening with our usual banter and playing video games like the friends we'd always been. There was no more talk of mysterious books or anything that had happened over the past few weeks.

Later that night, I thought about Teddy. My dad noticed something different about him. The only thing I noticed was he didn't care anymore. He didn't call after he got home to get more information about the book and act like my nagging big brother. We were the same age, but that's how he always acted.

Maybe I'd become just a stupid girl to him, and boys didn't hang out with girls so much after a certain age. At least that's what my dad told me before the start of my sixth-grade school year. He wanted to prepare me in case that was the year my friendships changed. "Nope. That won't happen," I'd said. "Once friends, always friends." At the time, I was right. Maybe now, two years later, it was actually happening. Teddy was drifting away.

On Monday, Cameron stopped me outside the gym before the pep rally. He was one of the more stylish of my classmates, always wearing the latest gear. You know, the new items in front of the store or the clothes displayed on mannequins. Whereas I proudly shopped the clearance racks for the deals. He wore a warmup suit in the red, black, and white school colors with shoes to match.

"Excuse me," several people stated, pushing past me.

"Come over here." Cameron pulled me away from the doors, so we weren't blocking the entrance. "Something is definitely going on with Theodore," he said in a hushed tone. "Like he's depressed or something. My cousin went through that."

"Depressed? He doesn't act that way around me. I would know if he were depressed." I shook my head. "I don't think so."

"Why not?"

I shrugged. "He doesn't look like it. He's not moping around or anything. Plus, that's not the Teddy I know, and I know him."

"Why does depression have to look like what *you* think it looks like? People can hide things."

"True, but I don't think he's depressed."

"I'm just telling you something's up, just like Justin tried to tell us at lunch. We're all on the basketball team. Maybe we see stuff you haven't. Check it out for yourself. If I were you, as close as you guys are, I'd check in on my friend." Cameron gave me a look almost like my dad would give when he says, "I mean it, Sheena."

"I've got to get to the locker room. They can't start without the star player," he said and pointed at himself.

I stood there watching him as he jogged away. What was I supposed to do? Tackle Teddy and yell in his face, "What's wrong with you? Why are you acting so weird?" followed by a slap across his face to snap him out of it?

Cameron turned and jogged backward.

Why was I still standing there?

"You look cute today," he said and turned back.

Embarrassed, I quickly turned toward the gym and ran smack into Chana.

"Why are you smiling like that?"

"I'm smiling?" I didn't realize it. I mean people smile while they walk, don't they?

"Hmm..." was all she said.

"I'm just happy about the pep rally. This is a big game. Steele is not going to beat us this time." I pulled her. "Come on, let's get a good seat."

We found seats high up on the bleachers. I stood looking for Ariel as the FPS, also the cheerleading squad, walked onto the floor in their red, black, and white uniforms.

"Did they shorten their skirts or something?" asked Chana. She tried to cover the eyes of the boy on the other side of her. He knocked her hand away.

The squad stood like statues, looking down with their hands at their sides. The music started, and I mean the entire gym went wild. I was even into it. Singing out on certain parts and cheering them on.

"Okay, Bradly!" Chana yelled. She led the routine. I had to admit, they were good.

I held up my phone and zoomed in on Bradly.

"You'll be her new bestie if you get some good shots for her to post."

"Nope, you've got that spot. But she'll like these."

The school mascot danced in front of them. He couldn't dance like the FPS. His movements were more funny than precise. I used to want to wear that cardinal uniform. I pretty much had bird legs anyway.

The cheerleaders left the floor and stood on the sidelines holding their pom poms. An announcement was made about the upcoming game. Then the basketball team ran out on the floor as their names were called. They dribbled and passed basketballs, running drills.

We screamed as loud as we could for Teddy. He held his hand up and then ran forward for a layup shot. I watched him bouncing a basketball between his legs. Unlike the other kids who wore t-shirts or sleeveless jerseys, he wore a long-sleeved black shirt. Actually, he wore the same shirt or one like it, every day, recently.

I leaned in toward Chana. "Does Teddy seem strange to you? I mean, like he's acting strange?"

She shook her head, but I noticed her watching him.

After the rally, Chana held me back as the kids around us descended the bleachers. "I was thinking. If you think something is wrong, do that thing to him."

"What thing?"

"Where you touch people and you can see stuff."

"I don't think I can."

"Why not?"

"I don't think I have that ability anymore. I've touched people and nothing happens."

"Were you trying to look into their lives?"

"No. But I wasn't trying to in the past when it worked, either."

"Well, you need to find out. Try it on someone to see if you still have it. That someone might as well be Theodore since you're all worried." Her voice took on a kiddie tone as if she were singing her favorite playground song:

Theodore and Sheena
Sitting in a tree
K-I-S-S-I-N-G!

"No! Stop it! Stop smiling," I said. "It's not like that."

"Oh, is it like that with Cameron?"

"Did we just meet? Do you not know how my father is?"

"You're right. Never mind."

10

I snuck up on Teddy in the hall. "Heyyyy…"

"Hey, Sheena. What's up?"

"Nothing." I touched his arm, but nothing happened. *Maybe the cloth of his shirt is in the way.*

"Okay," he said slowly. "Let me borrow your headphones."

"Take them but meet me right here tomorrow to give them back."

"You're giving them up overnight? Cool!"

I held out my hand. "Shake on it." *Ooh, that was good thinking.*

Teddy grabbed my hand, and I braced myself expecting to see a door open behind his eyes. Any minute, I'd know everything that was going on with him.

"Sheena?"

I stared at him.

"Can I have my hand back? What's wrong with you? Why are you standing there like that?"

"Nothing. I just remembered something I have to do." I backed away, feeling my heart sink. I saw nothing.

I went looking for Chana, and found her outside of class, scanning the hall, looking for me.

"Oh my gosh, I thought you wouldn't make it before the bell."

"I think it's gone," I told her, almost in tears.

"What?

"The gleamerism. I don't have it anymore."

"You say that like it's an illness or something."

"That's not what I meant. It didn't work with Teddy. I didn't feel or see anything."

"But that's a good thing, right?"

"No," I said as I walked past her, entering the classroom. There was an underlying sorrow I didn't want to discuss, because the Teddy I knew would never have allowed me to hold his hand like that. He knew me and would have known what I was doing.

Chana followed me inside and sat at a desk next to mine. "If nothing is happening, maybe it's because everything is going to be okay."

I didn't respond. I wanted to believe that was true. I mean, I really wanted to believe the Murk was out of my life for good, and that my friends and family were safe. But deep within me somewhere, I was unsettled. Teddy should have realized I was up to something. And if we were safe, why was I still having nightmares?

My dad and I drove separate cars into the parking lot of a shopping plaza. He parked in the center of the lot, and I pulled into one of the parking spaces in front of a sandwich shop entrance. I looked back at my dad's car and noticed two white vans pulling into the lot. They parked on either side of my car.

For some reason, I knew the guy in the van on the left was going to grab me when I got out of my car. I opened the door, and he came around the side of the car, eyes glowing red. I ran to get to my dad, only I couldn't run fast enough so I jumped into the air, just avoiding the guy's grasp. I flew toward my dad, but I kept rising and couldn't direct myself. My dad frantically waved his arms at me, seeing me in the air. I'm flying wildly, arms flailing, and screaming while rising so high that I enter space.

Suddenly, I accelerated toward the center of the solar system. And just before I plunged into the hot gasses of the sun, I stopped. Plasma or something shot out at me. This part happened in slow motion. I saw it coming, and I don't know why, but I reached for it. It filled my hand and I pulled it to my heart. It disappeared there, inside me.

Instantly, I was back in the sky flying toward my dad, and he jumped and grabbed me out of the air. He held me to him, and I told him about the men. Of course, he knew already because he saw everything. He just wanted to get me out of there.

I awoke and ran to tell my dad about my dream. He'd fallen asleep in the family room on the couch. "Daddy," I said as I stood over him. "Daddy, wake up." He opened his eyes and smiled up at me. His arms raised, and I moved in closer for his embrace. But he choked me. I fought to pry his hands from around my neck. His pupils were huge and glowing red. I tried to cry out but couldn't make a sound, as his hands grew hot like fire.

I sat up in my bed, gasping for air and holding my neck. This time I was really awake. I threw my legs over the side of my bed, ready to charge down to my parent's bedroom. But my mom ran into my room first. "Sheena, what's wrong? I heard you scream."

She sat on my bed facing me while rubbing my arms. My eyes teared. "Mom, it's starting again."

She moved in closer, looking worried. "You've been having nightmares for a while. What is it that's starting?"

"The Murk," I whispered.

11

"*H*oney, tell me what happened."

I cried into my mom's shoulder. I'd known it wasn't over with the Murk after Luke was arrested. But I didn't want it to start up again. Not this soon. I wasn't ready. Could I at least turn sixteen or something first? This was too much for a middle schooler.

"Did you see an angel? Did an angel tell you that? Is that what happened?"

I wiped my eyes. "I saw... I saw..." I'd just remembered the part where I touched the sun. *What was that? What did it mean?*

"Sheena, don't try and talk about it now. I can barely make out what you're saying between sobs. Here, lay back. I'm right here. You have nothing to worry about."

I laid back on my mom, remembering every bit of the dream, as she stroked my hair. There was a lot to be worried about. The Murk was coming for me. *But why was my dad involved? Were they going to try to use him against me? Not my dad. There's no way.*

Eventually, I fell asleep in my mom's arms. When I awoke, she was still right there holding me, and I was so glad.

"Belinda," my dad whispered from the door.

I felt my mom moving under me, and I rolled over so she could get up. She left the room and talked softly in the hall. I suddenly sat up. "Nana. I need to talk to Nana."

I searched my nightstand and then under my pillows for my phone. Her phone rang and rang, but she didn't pick up. *Nana, where are you? Pick up, pick up, pick up.*

I disconnected the call and laid back against my pillows.

"Sheena," my mom called. "Get dressed for school. Your dad and I are going to the hospital."

"Why? What happened?"

"Nana fell."

"She fell? I'm going with you."

I dressed quickly. I know I washed my face because I remember the tingle from the acne treatment foam. But I don't think I brushed my teeth. And I didn't touch my hair.

Before anyone could fuss about me taking too long, I grabbed my coat and boots. In true Sheena fashion, as I ran to the car, I slipped down the porch steps.

"Sheena! Are you okay?" My mom's muffled voice came from behind the scarf that covered her mouth from the cold. She reached out to help me up as my dad scraped the ice from the windshield. My bottom hurt, but all I cared about was getting to Nana.

At the hospital, the doors to the emergency room lobby slid open and my mom hurried to the counter to ask about Nana.

"Can't we just go back?"

"No. We have to speak to someone first."

An attendant gave us visitor passes and took us to Nana. Each cubicle of a room was separated by curtains. I burst in. "Nana, are you okay? What happened?"

"Glory be, look at you. Stop worrying, Sweetie. Nana's okay. I just took a little tumble."

"A tumble?" My mom and I exclaimed in unison.

"I tripped."

"What were you doing? Running?"

"Me, running? I don't think so. I'm about as slow as molasses running up a hill." She laughed. "No. I just tripped stepping up on a curb. I thought—" she abruptly stopped talking.

"Nana?"

"Mama?" said my mom after kissing Nana on the forehead.

"—I thought I saw someone I knew, and I wasn't paying attention to where I was stepping after getting my mail from the mailbox."

I expected Nana to say the Murk was involved, but she didn't. I was so relieved that that's all it was.

My dad walked in and his dark figure behind me scared me. He placed his hand on my shoulder. "You are so jumpy, lately."

That dream messed me up. Now, wherever I went, I was back to looking out for the Murk. I mean its avatars, the triplets—the boy and the two girls. If it was truly all starting up again, I expected them to start up with their threats again.

But, If I'm not a gleamer anymore, why is the Murk even bothering with me? And how did I lose the gleam? When I died and came back? Or was it taken away because I doubted myself so much? Did I fail the angels somehow? Or is it heaven? Did I fail heaven? But I had done good, I thought. I fought against the fear. Luke was incarcerated. How could it be taken away?

When Nana's doctor walked in, the room became too crowded, so I used that as an excuse to step outside. I walked down the hall and stood in front of the elevators. There was nothing stopping me from going up to NICU. Why was I feeling so anxious about it?

The last time, I was there with Mr. Tobias. He'd shown me them—the guardians. And if I couldn't see them this time, it would truly mean I wasn't a gleamer anymore.

I boarded the elevator. When the doors opened, I faced the security door that led into NICU. *All you have to do is close your eyes and focus. When you open them and look through the glass, they'll be right there in all their glory.* There's one for each child, Mr. Tobias had said.

I walked up to the door and peeked through the glass pane. *Focus.* I closed my eyes and realized I was shaking. I clasped my hands together and thought of Mr. Tobias and how he told me, *"You're blocking yourself—limiting your vision. There is a deeper reality than what is. Close your eyes and concentrate. Open your eyes with an awareness of what is really happening around you."*

I became very still, and just when I felt like I was no longer aware of my surroundings, I inhaled deeply and exhaled, opened my eyes, and looked through the window.

Nooooooo...

12

A nurse walked across the corridor, a couple walked into
a room, and a man with a long beard stood outside a
window looking in at his infant. That's all I saw. There
were no guardians.

I sighed heavily. I'd lost it. After complaining so much
about being a gleamer, it was finally gone. But now I just
wanted it back.

"I'm sorry I acted like that. I should've been grateful for
the gift. Forgive me." That's all I could think to say. I
turned away from the door and walked back to the
elevator.

As I reached out to push the button, the doors slid open.

"Nurse Javan!" I gasped and wrapped my arms around him.

"Whoa, heyyyyy…"

"I'm sorry. I'm so sorry. I don't know what just got into me." I spoke really fast as I backed up, happy to see him, and smiling huge on the inside. He looked the same as always: caramel skin like mine, short curly hair, and grey scrubs.

"I-I was just going to find my mom. Do you remember me?"

"How could I possibly forget you?"

"Is this a sign? This is a sign, right? You being here? Remember? Because I was like, 'Who are you?' and you were all, 'I am Javan, I am Mr. Tobias, I am Nana, I am…' Remember?"

Nurse Javan laughed. "I have no idea what you mean, but it's nice to see you again. You always say the funniest things. What were you doing up here? Do you have a sibling in NICU?"

My heart dropped about a thousand feet into a pit. "No. I just look through the window."

"Oh, gotcha. You come up to pray for the babies?"

"Uh…" That pit became a bottomless chasm. Why hadn't I ever thought to pray for them, knowing they were all ill? *Wait a minute. That's what Mr. Tobias was doing when Teddy thought he'd fallen asleep.*

Nurse Javan looked through the window. "Many of the babies are pre-term, which means they were born early.

Many have low birth weights, like less than five pounds. Some have serious health conditions."

"I was less than five pounds."

"Then if you were born here at Hackley—"

"I was."

"Then you were probably in this same unit. They can use all the prayer they can get, and so can their parents."

I felt like such an idiot. A selfish one, only thinking about my own problems. "You're right. I-I think I would like to pray for them. I mean, I'm going to pray for them."

Nurse Javan used the scanner and unlocked the door. "Come in."

"Wha-what?"

"So you can pray for them."

"I can do that?"

"Just stay right here and I'll come back for you."

I didn't mean pray here. Is he going to watch me? I can pray anywhere, right, like at home? Teddy is not going to believe this.

Nurse Javan went to the nurses' station and came back. He brought me to a window, and I looked in over babies in incubators with parents beside them. A mom reached her hand in and held her baby's hand. The man with the beard turned away from his wife and cried.

Nurse Javan stepped back away from me. I was glad he'd given me a little space. I closed my eyes and prayed for all of them. Healing for the infants and strength and comfort for their parents. For a moment, I felt the love that mom felt as she held her baby's hand, as well as the pain she felt. Then a peacefulness filled me. I didn't care if I could see the guardians or not. I only wanted the babies to get well.

Loud beeping came from the room. Nurses ran in. It was the man with the beard's child. I ran up to the window with my hands on the glass, my nose almost smashed against it, as they worked on the child. I closed my eyes and prayed again, earnestly.

When I looked in the room again, I stumbled back a few steps, almost blinded by the glow. There they were. A guardian for each child, and they nodded toward me, glowing a white blue. Almost transparent.

A voice next to me whispered. "May your vision be true." I turned to Nurse Javan. He was gone.

"Sheena, where have you been? I don't like you running off like that, especially now," my mom fussed.

"Now? Why? What's going on now?" asked my dad.

"Nothing, Jonas. Strange people are everywhere."

"You know my daughter can be a little overprotective, Jonas," said Nana.

"But she's hardly ever wrong," my dad said and winked at her.

"Mom, I was praying for the babies in NICU." For the moment I was as happy as could be, and it showed. I was still a gleamer. You would've thought it was my birthday, the way I grinned.

My mom and dad looked surprised. "That was sweet of you to do, Sheena."

"That's my baby," said Nana, smiling at me.

My dad helped Nana with her coat. "You're glowing," she said with a wink.

That was that proximity glow Mr. Tobias spoke of.

"Mama, I'm going to need you to be more careful," my mom told Nana.

"I *am* careful, Belinda."

"I know, but just pay attention to where you're going, please."

Nana shot her an irritated look. "You two go and get the car. Sheena can stay here with me."

A nurse rolled Nana down to the ER entrance where we sat looking out the door for my parents.

Nana watched me over her glasses. "Do you want to talk about it?"

"How did you know—never mind. I thought I wasn't a gleamer anymore, so I went to find out."

"What made you think that?"

"I didn't feel like I was."

"You have to believe, even when you can't see it. Do you stop being a kid when you don't feel like one?"

"No."

"You won't always feel like a gleamer, that doesn't mean you aren't."

"But I haven't gleamed lately, either."

"Maybe you're not supposed to. Although, I sense—"
Nana turned away from me and looked toward the parking
garage, deep in thought.

"What are you sensing, Nana?"

"A shifting. Something near you is off balance."

"You can see that?"

"I discern it."

"Tell me what it is because the Murk is back and if it's
back—"

"Back? What makes you think it ever left?"

13

*W*hy *did I think the Murk had left? Was that a trick question?* Just as I was about to ask Nana about it, my dad pulled up out front, and my mom rushed inside to help push Nana's wheelchair out. When we were almost to the car, a breeze blew over us. It's winter, so you expect cold breezes, but this was just one hot gust, like from a furnace.

Nana and I looked at each other and turned, hearing the hospital doors slide open. "Mom, stop." We all looked back toward the hospital. "Why did the doors open?" No one was anywhere around the entrance.

"I don't know," my mom said.

Nana didn't respond. The doors then closed and opened again. Still, no one was there.

"What was that, Nana?"

She looked at her watch. "Nothing I would worry about."

My dad walked up to us as the hospital valet walked out of the building and jogged toward the parking garage. "Come on, Mama Val," he said as he helped her up and into the backseat.

"Yes, I need to get home."

"Why can't you come to our house?"

"I think that's a good idea," said my mom. "Stay a few days."

"Now is not a good time."

"Why isn't it a good time?" I whispered in the backseat.

"Don't you worry, Sweetie. I'll be fine."

"Nana, that wasn't an answer."

She turned to me with a straight face. "I think you need to get to school. You still have almost a half-day left. Isn't there something of importance going on this afternoon?"

How did she know that?

Students quickly ran out of the media center as soon as the bell rang. I think half of them had been counting the seconds, waiting to make their escape. The last period of the day tended to be that way.

When I arrived at the media center, Rebecca saw me and patted the chair next to her for me to join her and the other bookworms in the front row. *Great.* We sat in an area the librarian had sectioned off from the aisles of books. Rows of chairs lined up in front of a huge screen and projector. The author, Stephen Woodruff, stood in front of us wearing a denim shirt, jeans, and a blazer. He looked like a professor.

What I'd read so far in his book led me to think he knew about the Murk. However, he didn't mention anything concerning the dark force. He mostly talked about his writing process and read a couple of excerpts, for examples, from his book.

Rebecca sat beside me squirming with anticipation of the question and answer portion of the visit. "Will there be a fifth book to the series?" she asked, hopeful.

"Well…" He looked around at all the faces in the area, building up the suspense. His eyes stopped on me for some reason. "Maybe."

Rebecca sank back in her seat. I was as disappointed as she was. Not because he might not add to the series, but because, the whole thing seemed a waste of my time. That is, until Mr. Woodruff ended the presentation with, "As you've likely read in my books, we'll end with the same salutation. May your vision be true. Thank you, everyone."

I stood with a look of shock on my face as everyone clapped. Only gleamers say, "May your vision be true." Would just anyone say something like that? I backed away and waited for the area to clear so I could get a one on one with the author.

"There you are," said Chana. "So that's Stephen Woodruff, huh?"

"You're not going to believe this," I whispered.

"You're right. I can't believe you didn't comb your hair today."

I touched my ponytail. "You can tell?"

"It's all wild looking. I can't believe you. Why didn't you?" She frowned.

"Because who cares. You've got to hear this!" My tone conveyed a harshness that I didn't mean, but I needed her to focus on what I was saying and not on my appearance.

"What? What did I miss?"

"Aww man, look."

A line formed to speak to the author.

"How are we going to get to talk to him? We need a notepad."

"Why? I'm on assignment."

"Yeah like you're some big-wig journalist. It's only the school newsletter."

"So what? At least I'll have experience for high school."

"What am I, your assistant?"

"That. Or you can let him sign your notepad like you want his autograph. How did you get in here, anyway?"

"I have my ways. Do you know what you're going to ask him?"

"I've worked out a few things, but—"

"Mr. Woodruff…" said a voice from the front of the line. "What about the dark force you wrote about in your book? Is that real or a metaphor?"

"Who is that?" Chana and I looked around the kids in line in front of us. "Move," said Chana to one of the girls. "Stop being rude."

"It's Ariel. Did you tell her about it?"

"No. Why would I?"

"Thank you for reading my book. It's fiction. But it's describing the fate of our youth. I mean, in a fictional sense." The author's eyes widened as he noticed Ariel's bracelet. "That's interesting. Where did you get it?"

"Thanks. My mom. So you're saying it isn't something we have to worry about in real life?"

He looked like he began to say something but changed his mind. "These are great questions. I can see you've given this quite a bit of thought. Good on you. Like I said before, it's fiction." Then he lowered his voice.

"What did he just say to her?"

"I don't know. They're both smiling, though."

"His head was angled down so I couldn't try to read his lips."

"When could you ever read lips? Ask her what he said."

"I can't. That was private."

"Yeah, but you know you want to know. And she'll tell you anything. Look, she's leaving. Go."

"But—"

"I'll hold your spot. Go."

I ran into the hall after her. "Ariel, wait up."

"Sheena…"

"Hey, I saw you talking to Stephen Woodruff just now. What did he say?"

"You were in there? I didn't even see you. How did you know about the author visit? Do you read his books?"

"I heard some girls talking about it. What did he say?"

"Oh, he said it's fiction. None of it is real."

"No. I mean he whispered something to you—unless it's private. You don't have to tell me—unless you want to."

"I don't mind telling you. He said, 'Remember everything your mother taught you.'"

"That's weird. Why would he say that?"

Ariel shrugged. "It's what he said. See you later, Sheena." She turned around and walked backwards as she spoke. "Let's hang out later. Okay?"

"Why not now?" I wanted to find out what else she knew about the author.

"I've got to do something real quick," she said as she backed away in that sort of skipping walk she has.

"Well?" said Chana, walking out of the library.

"What's that?"

"Stephen Woodruff's autograph."

"You really got it?"

"I had to. I held your place in line. Then it was my turn. If I'm lucky, this bad boy will get me some extra credit points in English. So what did Ariel say?"

"I think he knew her mom. Something about remembering what her mother taught her. Chana, don't make it obvious, but turn around slowly."

Chana made it seem she was looking for something and turned to see Stephen Woodruff at the library entrance.

"Is he watching us?"

"I don't know. Maybe he was waiting because the librarian told him he'd be interviewed for our newsletter, but no one actually *did* it."

My hand flew to my mouth. "Oh my gosh, I forgot. And he's leaving."

"Well, follow him. Go, go go." Chana and I ran down the stairs. "Why is he walking so fast?"

"Maybe he has somewhere to be, like another school."

We ran past a window. "Wait, look." Outside, a car pulled up. A woman stepped out and stopped him.

"Is that Nana?"

They embraced.

"Whoa, what's going on here?"

14

I didn't confront Nana. I continued with my day as usual until Chana Facetimed me later. All the get well cards and notes from my locker were on my desk in front of me. I shared the funniest and kindest ones with her.

"Listen to this one. 'If you don't get better, I'll drown you.' Who leaves that kind of—"

Chan cut me off. "Are we not going to discuss the big white elephant in the room?"

"Which would be what?"

"Nana and Stephen Woodruff hugging it out in the parking lot and leaving together. That's why he was in such a rush, his ride was there."

"There's nothing to discuss. An old friend flew into town and they met up after his author visit."

"That's what Nana told you?"

"She didn't have to."

"I am totally unequivocally appalled!"

I laughed at her choice of words. "Why are you appalled?"

"Because investigating is what you do, and you're not trying to find out what's going on? You know Nana should've been at home taking it easy after falling this morning. Nope I'm not going for it. Something's wrong. What is it?"

"Nothing." I watched her lean forward. "What are you doing?"

"Putting on my boots. I'm about to walk over there and tackle you. In the snow. At night."

"You wouldn't make it two feet out of your house. I *am* going to ask her about it, just not right now."

"Call her, and then go and ask you mom about my sleepover."

"What sleepover?"

"The one I'm about to beg my parents to let me have. They may take pity on me since my best friend almost died."

My mom didn't feel good about me going to Chana's sleep over. She sat at her vanity twisting her wet hair in sections.

"You might try to crawl into her parent's bed in the middle of the night."

"Mom, yuck, no. You don't understand."

"What don't I understand, Sheena?"

"It doesn't work unless it's *your* bed. Or maybe Nana's."

"What doesn't work?"

"I don't know." I shrugged. "The power over monsters. We're going to be up all night anyway."

She pointed her comb at me. "You're saying my bed has power over monsters?"

"Yes, it does." I thought for a moment. "How about either allowing me to go to the sleepover or..."

"Or?"

"Letting me have a dog." I looked hopeful. It wasn't the way I wanted to ask, but I would accept whichever she agreed to.

"Go and pack for your night."

Chana plopped down onto her floor pillows with a bag of potato chips. We both wore our cherry patterned, pink footed pajamas, and pulled the hood over our heads.

"What are you all deep in thought about? You're supposed to be watching the movie."

I swirled a straw in my milkshake. "My mom won't let me get a dog."

"What are you, five years old—ready to cry because you can't have a dog? Do you know what you'd be doing right now if you had a dog?"

"Enlighten me."

"Outside walking him when the windchill factor is ten below."

"Okay, maybe I didn't think that part out."

"Turn that up some. I want to hear what she says. This is getting on my nerves. I think I could write a better script—at least it would be more realistic."

"You should try."

"Look at them staring at each other. Neither of them wants to break up, but they won't say anything. Instead, they just stare at each other. Sheesh, just be honest with people already."

"You mean like you?"

"I'm as honest as they come."

"Oh? Tell me who you are, really, Chana."

She flicked her hand up at me like she was shooing me away. "Whatever."

Her phone dinged.

"Who's that?"

"Cameron."

"Ooh, you and Cameron? Wait, I said that without thinking. Can guardians do that?"

"Stop with that guardian stuff. And not me and Cameron. *You* and Cameron."

"There is no me and Cameron."

"Then you need to tell *him* that."

"Why?"

"Haven't you noticed? Where is your head at? It's upsetting Theodore."

"Why would Teddy be upset?"

Chana spun around looking for something, reached for a magazine, and knocked me over the head with it. "You are so oblivious."

"Oblivious to what?"

"I can't right now with you."

"Yes, you can, can, can," I sang as I jumped up, doing a can can dance. I think I'd had too much sugar.

"Wow. I never thought I'd see this. You've lost your cool card."

"Did I ever have one? He keeps calling. Pick up. I won't listen." My dancing transitioned from can can, to Irish stepdance, to tap. *Definitely too much sugar.*

"He's Facetiming."

"Well answer it."

"Chana, what's up, girl?"

"Look who's here." She turned the camera toward me. I waved.

"What are you guys doing?"

"You can't tell by these onesies we're wearing? It's a sleepover."

"That's what's up. We're on our way."

"No, you're not. We who?"

"Me and my cousin, Corey." He turned the camera. It was the boy that helped fight to rescue Dingy.

"No."

"Why not?"

"It's late and we're in our pj's. My dad would have a conniption."

"Hey, what's that paper?" I asked.

"Nothing."

"His drawing," said Corey.

"What are you drawing?"

Corey snatched the page and held it up.

"It's for my graphic novel I'm writing."

"I didn't know you could draw. Let me see another one."

"There's a lot to learn about me, I'm amazing."

"Says who? Is that an angel with muscles? Cameron, you better not be—"

"Here's another one," said Corey just as Cameron tackled him.

We laughed, watching them. Corey threw him to the side and held the now crumpled page up, just as Cameron snatched it.

"Hold on. I saw curly hair. Was that me? Cameron, you better not be writing a novel about—"

"I'm not."

"Seriously, don't."

"I said I'm not."

"Are you guys coming to church Sunday?" asked Corey.

"Your church?

"Yeah."

"He's been a changed man since that night he helped us. He's not even dealing anymore."

Corey punched Cameron. "What are you bringing that up for?"

"You showed my drawing." Cameron looked back at the screen. "He wants to be an investigator and help find missing children now. He's been going to my church too. You should come."

"Maybe."

"Well, umm..."

"Just ask her," said Corey.

Chana glanced at me. "Ask her what?"

"Will I see you at the dance?"

"Yes, you will," she replied, while putting the camera on her face. "What were you calling for anyway?"

"Oh yeah. Theodore. Man, you better check on him. He's getting worse. I'm going to his house tomorrow. You guys in?"

"We're in. Now, we've gotta go. Pizza and hair dye calls."

"Hair dye?" I asked as she ended the call. "That's the surprise you had planned for tonight?"

"What? It washes out. It's not permanent." She held up two jars. "Green or purple. Which do you want?"

I sat on a stepstool in Chana's bathroom as she colored individual strands of my hair. "Don't do too many or my mom will flip."

"It literally washes right out." Black licorice hung from the corner of her mouth as she spoke.

I watched her in the mirror. "I still don't know how you eat that stuff. It's all pepperminty and everything."

Chana dangled the licorice in my face, and I pushed it away. She placed it back in her mouth, and when she wasn't expecting it, I snatched it out and threw it in the trash. I fell over laughing at the shocked look on her face.

"Really, Sheena?"

"It's not like you don't have a whole bag of them."

A half hour later, we were done. I leaned in toward the mirror studying my reflection. The green and purple highlighted strands of hair stood out against the dark brown ringlets. "It's funky. It has that eighties vibe. And you know we like the eighties."

Chana pulled her hair up on the sides, so it looked like she had a purple and green highlighted mohawk. "Yes, we do, but you more than most. Please don't start in with your eighties tunes."

"Shall we work on our dance moves for the dance now? You know I have a playlist ready."

"Ha! No! Did you bring the book?"

"It's in my bag."

"I was joking. Do you keep it on you at all times now?"

I laughed. "No. I thought I may want to read it. Rather, *try* to read it."

"Oh."

"Only because I may have trouble sleeping." I looked away. "That's been happening lately." Chana didn't know about my nightmares.

"You'll sleep fine here."

"You think so?"

"Yep."

Chana was right. After pepperoni pizza, a banana split, three brownies and several gummy worms, I did sleep well. In fact, I think I fell asleep before Chana for once.

I awoke just before dawn. Chana snored softly to the left of me. I reached for my backpack, but it wasn't where I'd left it. Chana kicked her leg in her sleep and hit my bag, near her foot. *There it is.*

Instead of spending the evening reading the Lumen—at least that's what I thought we'd do—we just hung out and had fun. I didn't even think about the Murk. But when I awoke, it all came flooding back.

I picked up my backpack. It felt light. I looked inside. The Lumen was gone.

I ran around the room, throwing things everywhere, searching for the book, and then found it had gotten pushed under the bed somehow. A book doesn't just crawl out of a bag. Chana had to have taken it out. Why did she have it? I clutched the Lumen to my chest as I glared at Chana. What was she keeping from me?

Either I could wait for her to waken or—nope, I need answers immediately. I grabbed Chana's shoulder. She always slept deeply, so I shook her hard. "Wake up, Chana! Wake up!"

"Scrabumble slu," she mumbled in her sleep.

I shook her again and held the book in her face. "Why did you take this? I know you hear me!"

Chana opened her eyes. "What's wrong, Sheena?"

"Why did you take this from my backpack?"

"Sheena, calm down."

"You can read it, can't you? What did you find? What are you keeping from me?" I opened the Lumen to the page Chana had bookmarked with a ribbon. "What's here? I know you know. Tell me."

She sat up. "I thought you've read it."

My voice climbed. "I can't make out all of it yet, and you know it. Just tell me!"

"Shh... lower your voice. Do you want to explain this to my parents when they come stomping down here because you woke them?"

It didn't stop my anger and hurt, but I listened.

"You've read it, but you didn't see it. Not like this."

Chana grabbed her phone and took four pictures of the page.

"What are you doing?"

She didn't respond. Instead, she uploaded the photos to her computer and turned and overlapped them. I stepped closer to the screen. The center where the corners overlapped became a star. "Is that—"

"It's Ariel's star. The one from her bracelet. You don't understand what this is..."

15

"What is it?"
"A key."

I knelt over Chana's desk, staring at the image. "A key to what?"

"This book is called the Lumen, right? Lumen—light—opening. Opening of light. Understand?"

"No."

"It's a key to what's to come, but part of it is locked."

"Why?"

"I don't know."

"You have to find out how to unlock the secret of it and find out more about Ariel's bracelet."

I snatched the book from her. "Why would you have to sneak it away to look at it? Why couldn't you have asked me or studied it with me?"

"I was awake and just wanted to look at it. Stop acting like I'm against you. You know I'm not."

"If you're being secretive, you are."

"What's wrong with you?"

"I don't know. Nothing. I just don't like you right now," I said, knowing I didn't mean it.

"Well, get over it. Anything I do is for your best interest, and you know it. Let's just get some sleep so we can meet up with Cameron later and see what's wrong with your other best friend that you haven't noticed."

My mouth dropped. "That I haven't noticed? Wow, that was real harsh, Chana."

"So was talking to me like I'm a thief."

"Yeah? Well that's why you have dried saliva on the side of your mouth."

Chana and I had gotten into disagreements before, but we always made up. This time was no different. All it took was a bump of the hip at brunch (we'd slept through breakfast) and we were back to the giggling and cackling— as her dad called it—that made her parents want to kick us out.

"You guys need to get out of the house. Is there enough snow for sledding?" asked her mom.

That's when we knew we were getting on her nerves.

Chana's phone rang. She looked up at me and jerked her head to the side. I followed her into the next room to take the call.

"*Skurrrp.* The fox has fled the coop. *Skurrrp.*"

"What does that mean? That doesn't even make sense. What is that sound supposed to be?"

"A walkie talkie."

"That's dumb. Just say whatever it is you're trying to say."

"Basketball practice is over. He's on the move."

"That's all you had to say in the first place. His house is not far from mine. We'll leave in ten."

Chana tossed me a sweatshirt. "All right, girl. Let's do this."

"Detective Sheena is on the case."

We were thankful it stopped snowing and the sidewalks were clear. The sun was shining, and the wind chill factor only took the temp down to 30 degrees. The next day, it would probably be five below.

Teddy's driveway had been shoveled but needed salt. Patches of ice were here and there from the street up to the house. Chana and I held on to each other to keep from sliding up the walk.

"Boo!"

Whoosh!

I fell forward but Chana caught me by the arm and pulled me back.

"Cameron!" I whisper-yelled, wanting to smack him for scaring me. He cracked up, but I wanted to strangle him.

"Stop playing. What are we doing?" asked Chana.

"Why are you guys asking me?"

"Because this is your mission."

"Let's see if he's home."

"He's not going to be himself if we do that. There's a window right there," said Chana.

"We're snooping?" I asked.

"If that's what you want to call it. I call it being concerned. Just go."

We knelt below the kitchen window, each peeking in every few seconds.

"Can you see anything?" asked Cameron.

"No."

"Listen..."

I covered my mouth and flinched, hearing Teddy's father. I had never heard him sound so angry. "How many times do I have to tell you?" he yelled.

"Did he hit him?"

"I don't know." We'd all ducked.

"He's still yelling."

"If he didn't, he's going to. We have to do something," said Cameron. Chana and I looked at him, surprised. Especially since he and Teddy always seemed to have a rivalry going.

Cameron peeked in the window.

"Where are they now?"

"They went to the back. Come on."

"No. It'll leave footprints in the snow. They'll know someone's been out here spying." I tried to peek in the window and heard their doorbell ring.

"Someone's here," I said as I ducked.

"Wait, where's Cameron?"

"Hey, man."

"Cameron?"

"What's going on?" Cameron asked.

Teddy lowered his voice. "You-you have to go. It's a bad time."

"Can you step outside for a minute?"

Teddy looked back at his dad and shook his head.

"I think you should. You look like you need to cool down. Just take one step forward," Cameron said with a grin as if he were Teddy's favorite person.

Teddy looked down. He stepped on the front porch with the door open behind him.

"If there's something you want to tell me, tell me quick. Just whisper it."

Teddy looked back at his dad again and lowered his head. "I'm not well."

"What do you mean?"

"I've been having bad thoughts."

"What kind of bad thoughts?" Cameron whispered back, his face now showing concern.

Teddy clenched his jaw and I wasn't sure he was going to reply. "Really bad thoughts." he said as he rubbed his arms.

"Theodore," his dad said, his voice testy.

"You need to go now," he told Cameron.

Teddy looked off to the side and saw me ducking at the corner of the porch.

"Take care of her," he told Cameron.

He backed up and closed the door.

We all stood shocked. *This is bad, this is really bad.*

16

Something was going to happen. I didn't know what or to whom, but I could feel it. I had chills and it wasn't from the cold. "We have to do something!"

Cameron took that as the cue he'd been waiting for and kicked the door before it fully closed.

Chana and I ran up behind him.

Teddy faced his father. They looked like two boxers in a ring facing off before the first round of the match.

"You better not lay one hand on him!" Cameron yelled.

Teddy's father looked confused.

Chana held her cell phone up. "You know my dad is a police officer, and I have him on speed dial," she threatened.

"I don't know what you kids think is going on here, but first of all, know that this is my house, and you need to leave."

"We're not going anywhere," I said.

Cameron picked up a golf club that leaned against the wall. "Theodore, you can leave with us."

"Is this a joke? Sheena, you know me. Theodore is not in any danger," his dad said. His voice was kinder as he spoke, and believable.

"I'm not sure what I know anymore, but the way you yell at him—"

"Did you hear what he said to me? No child should ever talk to his parents that way. I don't know what's gotten into him, lately."

Chana and I glanced at each other.

"So what are we doing, what are we doing?" whispered Cameron in a nervous sing-song way.

"He's not leaving, so we need to go," said Chana.

"Yes, go," Teddy agreed. It was the first thing he'd said since we'd rushed in.

Cameron set the gulf club down and backed out with his hands up. Chana followed, and then me.

"Teddy, we'll be outside waiting for you. You need to pray about this," I said before leaving.

"You pray. I don't believe in anything anymore," he said as he closed the door in my face.

I stood there staring at the door until Chana pulled me away. What happened? Where was my friend because that was not him?

Chana, Cameron, and I waited on the sidewalk a few minutes until we couldn't take the cold anymore, scarves covering our faces, gloved hands stuffed in our pockets. "He's not coming. I thought he might change his mind. We should just go."

"Yeah, I'm out," said Cameron as he turned to leave and then turned back. "I'm sorry, Sheena. I know this was my idea."

"You didn't do anything to apologize for. We'll see you later."

I watched him jog away. Chana tugged at my arm. I stared at her eyes over her scarf. I waited. I mean, she's an angel. Couldn't she do something?

"What?" she asked.

I shook my head and walked away.

That night, I awoke startled. It felt like someone shoved me.

"Sheena, what—You're in here again? I thought that was over," my dad fussed. "Bee, we've got to start locking that door."

The doorbell chimed.

"Jonas, someone's at the front door," my mom yawned out.

He got up and looked out the window. "It's your mother."

"What mother?" she asked, groggily.

"How many do you have?"

My mom sat up. "Mama's here? She has a key, why won't she use it?"

"Maybe so she won't scare the living daylights out of us like someone else I know."

"Sheena, get up. Go get in your bed."

I scooted off the bed, but I didn't go to my room. I followed my parents. We hurried down the stairs like kids rushing down to open gifts on Christmas morning.

My dad opened the door and guided Nana inside. "Hi, Nana," I said as I hugged her, freezing coat and all.

My mom hugged her next. "Mama, what are you doing out this late?"

"You only come out in the middle of the night like this when you've had one of your feelings, Mama Val. What are you feeling tonight?" my dad asked with a smirk while taking her bag and coat.

"Well Jonas, those feelings are often warnings, and I can't ignore them," she replied, matter-of-factly and turned to me. "It's about your friend, Sheena."

"*My* friend?"

My dad yawned. "Which one?" He never believed Nana's 'feelings.' That's the spooky stuff he talked about.

"Theodore."

His eyes widened. "You too?"

Why could everyone see it except me?

"Is something going on with Theodore, Sheena?" my mom asked.

"It's bad. I didn't know. I mean, can a person hide abuse to the point that their best friend can't even see it?"

My dad walked toward me. "What kind of abuse?"

"Like verbal. Maybe physical too, but I didn't see that."

He rubbed his chin. "I was afraid of that."

"How did you know?"

"I've seen it before. I'm going over there."

"You can't."

"He's a good kid. The way we talk to our children becomes the voice inside them. This could ruin him."

"He says he's having bad thoughts. Can we do anything? I don't know how to help him."

"Sheena, we've had this conversation before. This is not a project for you to take on. I can see it all over your face. Your dad and I will figure it out, okay?" She turned to Nana. "Mama, you know I'm not letting you go back out tonight, so let's get a bed ready for you."

"I'll room with Sheena." Nana studied me. She grabbed my shoulders. "Let's see if we can't get you back in your own bed."

"How did you know that?" I threw my mom a look of shock. She shrugged. I was totally embarrassed. "What ever happened to what happens in this house stays in this house? Sheesh," I mumbled as Nana turned me toward the stairs.

"You go on up," my dad told my mom. "I'm going to stay down here for a while. He seemed just as upset about Teddy as I was.

"Mama Val, you know there is a thing called phones that we use when we want to tell someone something important?"

"Hush, Jonas," Nana joked as we climbed the stairs. Once in my bedroom, she looked at my bed and walked around the room, looked in the closet and moved the hangers around, searching behind my clothes. She even opened the hamper. Next, she slid my curtains back and looked out of the window. "Looks like a pretty safe place to me."

"It is for now." I knew nothing would happen as long as Nana was there. She could defeat any monster.

I pulled the trundle from below my bed and grabbed an extra pillow and blanket from the closet. Since we were up, I wanted to ask Nana all the questions I'd avoided asking her. Like about Stephen Woodruff. But Nana laid down and I mean she fell asleep as quick as a whip, as she would say. She didn't even ask to see the Lumen. Why wouldn't she? My guess was she already knew everything that was in it.

When I finally fell asleep, I dreamed as vividly as usual. Black lava-like sludge came after me and Nana. It flowed through a building, and a guy appeared to help us, telling us what to do. He told us what to say and gave us three objects to hold up when the sludge showed up again. It didn't work. We ran, and doors opened down a long hallway. The guy appeared again in each. He was the sludge the whole time. He'd given us what to do to let him in. Then the house we were in flipped over into Lake Michigan. We lost.

I awoke terrified. Nana sat watching me. I jumped up and she hugged me to her.

"Tell me," she said.

I told her everything I'd dreamed.

"Hmm... Your dream is clear to me, but you don't see it."

"What does it mean?"

"You're going to have to open your eyes and see."

"Please, Nana. No more riddles. You have to tell me more than that."

"How strong have you been feeling lately?"

"Not very strong."

"Have you asked for help?"

I looked down at my hands in my lap.

"Sheena, you are a gleamer. Your strength comes from above," she said as she pointed at the ceiling.

Nana held my face in her hands. "Every speck of light has a meaning. Every ray of light has a destination and a purpose. It is already determined. And it does exactly what it was created to do. That light pierces through every dark place. Capture that light."

She waited for my response. I wiped my eyes. "What in the world does that mean?"

Nana laughed. "Glory be. You'll know soon enough."

17

*M*usic blared and the bass pounded, rattling my bones and driving my heartbeat. With each thump, my excitement rose. I loved the energy the music gave the room. As I entered the cafeteria—now void of tables—turned dance hall, I looked around at the students standing along the walls and those in the center of the room showing off their style of the latest dances. It was too dark to really recognize anyone from afar. Sound-activated lights threw a kaleidoscope of color over everything. Everyone I did recognize looked a hundred times better than they did at school, in their new outfits and hairstyles.

"Sheena! Girl, you look so cute," said Bradly. I posed for her, showing off my brightly colored clothing: leggings, leg warmers, poofy skirt and lots of bangles. I was very 'Girls Just Want to Have Fun'-ish.

"Look at *you* though." Bradly was covered in lace. "You look—you look grown."

"I know right? My dress isn't too short, is it? I'm Madonna, 1984."

I couldn't even figure out how she'd walked out in the cold like that. Her coat must have been floor length. "Did your parents see it?"

"Yeah."

"They didn't object to it?"

"Nope."

"Then I guess it isn't."

"That's what I'm saying. Where's Chana?"

"I don't know. She said she would meet me—"

"Ah-hem..." Chana said and spun around.

"Now that's how you make an entrance. *Pretty in Pink*, right?"

"Don't hate, Bradly, it's not a good look for you." She looked behind her. "Girls, *that's* how you make an entrance."

We were not the only ones watching her. A few boys watched Ariel walk in also. She looked beautiful—cloned right from a 1980s valley girl, with neon pink tights and a tutu, neon cropped top and neon earrings, and a big polka dot bow tied around her hair like mine. I had given her the idea.

"Wow, Ariel."

"Too bad I don't look like this every day, right?"

"At least you and I are following the theme," I laughed.

"I don't think everyone got the same memo. *Bradly*. The dance is eighties themed, not a costume party. A third of the kids in here are Michael Jackson," said Chana.

"Well, we're still eighties," she quipped. "Let's mingle."

The four of us walked around the gym together.

"Whup," was the sound that came from Ariel as we passed a girl and boy kissing on the back wall behind a group. Like really kissing, like that's not a peck, but a kiss-kiss. I pulled her. "Come on, Ariel. Your eyes are too innocent to see that. It's gross anyway."

I looked back at the couple. To my surprise, it was Rebecca, one of the bookworms. With her hair all spikey and her face pressed against some boy's. *She has a boyfriend?* She definitely had more of a life than I had. You never really know someone. Chaperones headed right for them and pulled them apart.

We walked around the gym, getting a look at everyone. Every once in a while, the four of us would stop and kind of dance together. I think that was a hint for the boys to ask us to dance. They stood along the walls watching mostly.

The DJ was awesome. It was like he could read everyone's mind on what they wanted to hear. Everyone except me. A beat started, and just from that intro, we heard a few screams. A girl ran up to Bradly and grabbed her arm. "Let's do it."

We gathered around Bradly's FPS, watching them do one of their dance routines. This one was even better than the one at the pep rally. I bounced and moved my shoulders a bit. I didn't want to get all sweaty. Ariel bounced alongside me. Although awkward, she knew their routine. That's when I recognized her movements. "Ariel, you're the school mascot? That was you in the Cardinal costume?"

She laughed. "You can tell?"

I nodded. "You're good at it."

"Not really. But it's fun."

I looked around. Someone needed to open a door. It was getting hot and stuffy in there. "Has anyone seen Teddy?"

"Not yet."

Cameron walked over. He stared at me but didn't say much. Ariel elbowed me. Finally, he asked me to dance.

"No. I don't think so."

"Go," said Ariel. "You're the only one who hasn't danced with anyone yet."

"I danced with you guys. Doesn't that count?"

"She means with a boy," said Chana.

I whined as Cameron pulled me away. "Nooo... don't make me do it."

Ariel pushed as Cameron pulled. The playlist wasn't my classic oldies music, where I moved any way I wanted. This was hip hop. I couldn't dance like Bradly and her crew, and I didn't just have fun with it like Ariel did, but I wasn't too bad. I looked over at Chana and she gave me a thumbs up. No one wants to look crazy in front of the whole school. I mean, I did practice in the mirror some. My mom watched me. She said I could dance, but moms think you can do anything.

Cameron, on the other hand, could *really* dance. I felt stupid out there with him. Perhaps he could tell. "Do this," he said. And I followed along, making swiping movements with my hands as I turned, mirroring what he did. It looked like we'd planned it. I heard a few cheers behind me.

I laughed and noticed a guy behind Cameron, swaying in the crowd. I looked away. When I looked back, he was gone. I kept dancing and laughing at myself when I messed up. Cameron wouldn't allow me to stop when the next song started. I didn't mind so much. I was having a good time. Then I noticed the guy again. He walked through the crowd, watching me. I stopped dancing. He had a wicked smirk on his face and nodded toward me.

"What's wrong?" Cameron yelled in my ear. He looked over his shoulder. Of course, he didn't see anything.

It was Drake, the Murk avatar. Right there in my school—around my friends—looking at me. Dressed in black, looking like a bad boy—the kind of boy girls seem to flock to. My eyes were locked to his. I couldn't turn away. They began to pull me, and I stepped away from Cameron.

"Oh, the dance is over just like that? You're just going to leave me on the dance floor?"

I couldn't respond. Drake backed up and I stepped forward until I found myself in the hall away from all the other students. I heard my name being whispered and I had to follow. He wasn't the Drake I remembered from before. He was stronger, willing me in his direction. Before I could turn the corner, hands grabbed my arms, pulling me.

Ariel blocked my path. "Where are you going? Did you need some air?"

I blinked hard, staring at her like I just recognized her.

Chana let go of my arms. "Where do you think you're going without us?"

"Home. I-I think I'm ready to go home." I pulled my phone from my pocket to ring my dad. "Are you guys staying? Do you need a ride?"

Ariel looked behind her in the direction Drake had gone.

"What's wrong, Ariel?

"Nothing. I thought someone was back there."

Chana followed her gaze. "I'm not ready to go yet, but I'll wait with you."

"I'm ready. I'll catch a ride with you," said Ariel.

My dad had no problem with me wanting to leave the dance early and arrived quickly. I'm pretty sure he thought that since I was ready to go, I wasn't hanging out with some boy. He playfully teased Ariel on the drive to her apartment. They laughed and joked back and forth like the family we'd become.

"What planet are you from?" my dad said, as Ariel giggled. "No one says that. No one even thinks like that, Martian child."

But I was quiet as we drove, looking out the window, up at the night sky, and behind us. Searching for the Murk. I had a feeling it wasn't far.

It came for me at my school. Would it follow me home? Was I still safe at home?

18

*M*y mom wanted to hear all about the dance.

"It was fun."

"But you didn't stay."

"The music was so loud. I got tired of the boom-boom-boom pounding in my ears."

She looked at me like I might not be telling her something. "Did you dance?"

"I killed it," I said with a huge grin. That was all she needed to hear. She looked pleased and hugged me.

"Now go and take that makeup off."

Although I expected it, I didn't have a nightmare that night. But I remained on edge about where the Murk might turn up next. I kept checking my phone, disappointed there were no messages from an angel giving me instruction. I needed to know what to do. Who was going to help me?

I tried to decipher more of the Lumen and then looked online to see if anyone posted any pictures from the dance. There were a few selfies, but that was it. I couldn't wait to go to school and find out what I'd missed.

***

"Have a good day," my mom said as I hurried out of the car. "Stay warm!"

No matter how fast I walked and how I bundled up, the frigid air ripped right through me. The crowd of kids walking into the school couldn't move fast enough for me. I shivered down the hall and passed a few kids who snickered.

What's their problem? Just as I reached my locker, I heard my name.

Ariel ran to me. "Did you hear? Did Chana tell you?"

Ariel knows about new gossip before me? Since when? "What happened?" I asked as I grabbed books off the shelf of my locker.

"There was a fight, and some kids were caught making out."

"So the usual."

Cameron rushed up the hall. "Sheena, I had nothing to do with it. Someone is spreading a rumor."

"What rumor?"

Cameron didn't get the chance to answer me. Teddy approached walking fast. Eyes narrowed and lips tight. He shoved Cameron and then punched him right in the jaw.

"Teddy!" I yelled as some boys pulled him away. "What the heck is wrong with you?"

"With me? What's wrong with him? I heard about last night."

"Will someone tell me what happened last night?"

"Or what didn't," said Cameron, holding his jaw and fighting for the boys who held him back to let him go. "I didn't start the rumor. I had no part in it. I'm not that guy. I would never do that to you."

"Do what to me?" I asked.

"Oh, stop acting so innocent, like you don't know," said one of the FPS. "We saw you."

"Saw me what?"

"Come from the gym by yourself. Cameron came from back there a few minutes later," she sneered with her head low and eyes throwing darts like at a bullseye. "You were trying to play it off like you weren't back there together, but I saw you."

"First of all, she never went near the gym," said Chana, arriving out of nowhere and stepping in front of me. I pulled her back. I could see where this was about to go. "Second of all. What were *you* doing back there, Teila?"

Teila rolled her eyes. She was like the pretty snob girl in all teen movies. Time slowed as she walked and flipped her hair. When it rained, somehow the sky was clear over her while the rest of us got soaked. Not really, but I think that sums her up.

"Cameron, tell them the truth!" Teddy exclaimed.

"What do you think I've been trying to do? I was not alone with Sheena last night—ever. Does everyone hear me?" he yelled. His eyes pleaded with me to believe he didn't start the rumor.

"And I wouldn't do a slutty move like that."

"Then why were you back there, Cameron?"

"I thought I saw her. I wondered where she was going, so I followed her. But when I turned back there, no one was at the end of the hall. It was like she disappeared."

"Well, how do you explain what I saw?" asked Teila.

"I don't have an explanation."

"Well I do. She's a—"

"I didn't expect to see you two in my office again this year, if ever." said Principal Vernon. He typed on a laptop and then pushed it aside.

"We didn't start it."

"How about telling me what happened, so I can figure out what level of punishment is warranted."

The P word. I'm going to be in so much trouble. My dad is going to cut all communication with Chana.

"Not without Big Mouth."

"Chana!"

"Sorry, sir. I meant, not without Teila. She could tell you anything if you meet with her alone. And you want the truth, right?"

Principal Vernon's assistant brought Teila in. She'd been sitting outside of the office waiting her turn. I was glad we were brought in first. Now Teila wouldn't get to put on her crying act.

"Teila. Tell me what happened and why you think I shouldn't suspend all five of you right now."

Cameron and Teddy sat on a bench behind us.

I gasped. *Not a suspension. Would he really suspend me?*

"She was spreading rumors," Cameron started.

Mr. Vernon held his hand up. "Let her speak."

She sniffed. "Around eight thirty last night, I saw Sheena come from the gym. A few minutes later I saw Cameron."

"And?"

"I told one person they were back there together."

"Were you?"

"No," Cameron and I replied at the same time.

"I was already gone. Ask Ariel. My father picked us both up before eight."

"But I saw you."

"I told you it wasn't me. Call my dad. He'll tell you."

I glanced over my shoulder at Teddy. He looked shocked.

"Why did you tackle her?" asked Principal Vernon.

"Because she got up in my face," said Chana.

"Theodore, why did you punch Cameron?"

"Because I thought the rumor was true."

"Why do you kids think violence is the only way to settle things? Did you see the amber alert? Three of your classmates were the last to get picked up from the dance. They never made it home. So while you're fighting about a rumor, think of those kids."

We all looked at each other. *Three kids have disappeared?* They had to be thinking what I was thinking, well, all except Teila.

I shot up out of my seat. "Please don't suspend us. I promise it won't happen again."

"So you're speaking for all of you?"

I looked at Teila and shuddered. If this was going to work, I had to include her. "Mr. Vernon, may I talk to you alone?"

He nodded and excused everyone. When he sat again his brows furrowed and he hesitated before speaking. "Okay, Sheena, what's really going on?"

UR N the clear, I texted everyone.

Later Chana asked, "How did you get us out of that?"

"I have a way with words."

"No. Seriously."

"I'm not kidding. I had to explain why each person was innocent. It wasn't easy, but I argued our cases well.

Principal Vernon thinks I'm going to make a great attorney."

Truthfully, my defense wasn't that hard. Cameron was innocent to the entire thing. I had to reveal what I thought may be happening with Teddy—which fortunately, Principal Vernon was going to check into. Teila may have seen someone else. I mean, most of the girls were dressed in pretty similar eighties garb. Chana was only defending me. "Like you were defending her last time, against Cameron in the cafeteria?" Principal Vernon asked.

"No. Well, kind of. But do you know what something like that can do to a girl's reputation? Not the boy's, just the girl's?" I replied.

Principal Vernon seemed to understand. No suspension, but if I wanted my classmates off the hook, I'd have to take detention on behalf of everyone involved. He thought I was going to say no. I could tell by the way he looked at me with his brows raised. It was my turn to take one for the team, I guess. It was better than getting suspended or having my dad freak out again.

I knew there was only one answer to what Cameron and Teila saw. The Murk. It made them think they had seen *me*. But why? Or was it really after Cameron, but Teila was there?

Second period had already started when I arrived. My teacher stopped me at the door. "Sheena, they want you in the media center."

"Who needs me?"

"I don't know, but you should hurry along."

The librarian pointed to the table and chairs near the computer stations. I walked over and stood there, surprised.

"Sheena Meyer?"

"Ye-yes."

"I understand you want to talk to me?"

"How—"

"I left the other day without my interview?"

"Uh, yeah. Okay." I was caught off guard and not sure of what I wanted to ask him in the first place. "It was kind of you to come back, Mr. Woodruff." I held my hand out, but he didn't shake it. *Okay. I guess he has a thing about germs.*

"What would you have used for your assignment if I hadn't?"

"Uh, stuff from your website—your author bio, and what I learned from your presentation."

He chuckled. "It sounds like you've got it covered. You don't need my help at all. Well—"

"How do you know my grandmother?" I couldn't believe myself sometimes. I blurted it out just like that.

"Oh. I didn't know I did. What a small world. Who is your grandmother?"

"Valerie. Valerie, that you left the school with that day."

He nodded. "Have a seat, Sheena."

I sat in the seat beside his.

"Valerie and I are old friends. What my bio doesn't tell you is I'm originally from Michigan. I haven't been back in some years."

"You came back just for your author visit?"

"That and other things. I don't expect to be in town much longer. Just as long as I'm needed."

"Needed?" I looked at his hands clasped together on the table and up at his face. Something about him reminded me of Mr. Tobias. It made me warm to him quickly. Like he wasn't exactly a stranger.

"If you have everything you need for your article, I guess I'll get going. I have to keep a promise to a friend and deliver a message."

We stood at the same time. Mr. Woodruff held his hand out, and I shook it. Everything in the library went out of focus. The colors melding until there was nothing. Time stopped. A window opened behind his eyes. I didn't see what was in front of me. I didn't see his future or his past. I saw Mr. Woodruff standing in light. He spoke to me.

"Sheena?"

"Yes?"

"You really are who they say you are."

"Who is that?"

"The last gleamer and a type-one."

"That's what I'm told."

Mr. Woodruff smiled. "Listen closely. What if I told you the key to humanity's destruction is our youth?"

"I don't know, but I'm listening."

"The key to humanity's salvation is also our youth. It is reaping season. The Murk is collecting children."

"How?"

"Through their pain."

"For what?"

"Destruction. It is building an army to destroy all hope."

"What can we expect?"

"How can I put this in terms you would understand? *The Hunger Games,* only worse."

19

"*A*re you okay?" Mr. Woodruff asked as he released my hand.

"Yes." I looked at the clock on the wall. Not a minute had passed.

"You look so surprised. Has no one told you of your destiny?"

"Does everyone know but me?"

He looked at me oddly. "Do you understand?"

"I-I think I do." I looked around and lowered my voice, "You're a gleamer. A different kind of gleamer. So your book *is* talking about the Murk."

He smiled as he picked up his laptop bag. For the first time, I noticed the glow of his eyes.

"Why did you reveal this to me?"

He pulled the strap over his shoulder. "Because I knew what you were as soon as I saw you." I figured he meant the gleam. "And it's starting."

———⁓⁓⁓———

I knew something was coming. I just didn't know it was this big—something that would call in other gleamers.

"May your vision be true," Mr. Woodruff said before leaving.

I walked back to my class in a daze and sat at my desk next to Ariel. *Reaping season,* I thought. The Murk was collecting kids and calling in those they'd taken and released—the ones they'd brainwashed already. But for what? "*The Hunger Games,* only worse," he'd said. I'd read the books and seen the movies. Kids going after kids—To kill them? My heart rate began to speed up. I glanced around at all the kids in the class. *What's going to happen to us?*

My teacher's voice was nothing more than an irritating hum as I was swept away by my thoughts. My eyes drifted to the window where I noticed the sky darkening. It wasn't the dreary look we were used to on a winter day. This was an unnatural darkness that was moving toward us, like the shadow from a giant ship.

I watched the window, trying not to be obvious like I was the last time I noticed something. I wondered if Mr. Woodruff had left the school grounds yet.

A shadow fell over the window. *Where is it going this time?*

I almost fell out of my chair as something slammed into the building. Those around me stared. A kid laughed like I was trying to be funny. Evidently no one else felt the room shake.

"What happened?" asked Ariel.

"I nodded off for a second, I think."

She pointed, "Like Theodore." His head was down on his desk. He didn't even try to hide he was sleeping.

"Sheena," Mr. Haleigha called from the front of the class. "Don't you have anything to say?" I looked behind him at the projector screen. The words Toxic Chemicals filled the screen in white with a blue cloud of smoke around them.

"I mean, this is a subject that usually gets you all in an uproar. Now is the time to say your piece."

I shook my head. "I'll pass." I had no idea what he'd been talking about. What a great time to not pay attention at all, right before you get called on.

"So there's nothing you want to say about the PFC's in our waters? Come on, Sheena. You have my permission. Let me have it. Let's rock and roll!"

Why does he say stuff like that?

Mr. Haleigha wasn't going to let it go. I had to say something. "Uh, okay…"

Everyone waited. Some kids turned toward me.

Make it good, Sheena. "Perfluorinated chemicals are not just in our waters, but because of *your* generation and your parent's generation, some form of it is in all of us and we didn't even have a choice in it. How is that fair?"

"Yeah!" said a boy near the front of the class. A few students applauded. I was glad the subject was on something I was passionate about.

Without fail, Mr. Haleigha responded. He always has a rebuttal ready. At least this time I didn't say something that would warrant a call to my parents. He turned and walked toward the projector. My eyes followed him as I shifted in my seat and then froze in place.

"Nooo…" I said under my breath.

"Yesss…" said Drake. How was he standing right there in my class? Tall and lean with ebony skin and high cheekbones, he walked around the room, talking. "Nothing's fair in this world," he said of my response to Mr. Haleigha.

I looked around at my classmates expecting them to react to him. But no one else could see or hear him. "You think because you and the healer teamed up—"

Healer? I glanced at Ariel. She looked up at her computer screen and back down at her textbook. I was glad she wasn't focused on me, otherwise she'd notice how I was shaking.

What healer? I knew he couldn't hear my thoughts, so I had to ask. "What healer?" I whispered.

"Did you say something, Sheena?" Ariel glanced over and whispered.

"N-no."

She looked up at Mr. Haleigha and back down at her screen. "Ignore him, Sheena," she said while picking up her stylus. "He has no power over you."

My mouth dropped. I couldn't believe what I was hearing. *Ariel can see him? Can she hear him?*

"Leave her alone," she said without looking up. "Now!"

"Now? Now what?" asked Mr. Haleigha.

"Uh, we've got to fix this, now!"

He smiled. "I like your enthusiasm, Ariel. But it's not that simple..."

Drake disappeared. The darkness faded away from the window. It felt like someone had loosened a tight grip on the air. I released my desk and stared at my beet red hands.

What just happened?

The bell rang. Ariel jumped up and grabbed her backpack like nothing happened.

"Ariel, wait. Come here." I pulled her off to the side, allowing other students to pass. "You did heal that bird that day at the church, didn't you?"

"Sheena, can we talk after school? I have a project to turn in. See you later," she said as she rushed out of the room.

How could she just leave like that? Didn't she know my mind was going crazy with questions?

I watched Ariel at lunch. She was no different than usual. Not that I expected her to talk about it in front of everyone. I couldn't eat, though, so I gave my lunch away. The jokers were happy to split it up between them.

After school do you think Ariel came looking for me? Nope. I had to search for her. She pranced down the hall, past the office, like we had never even had a conversation earlier.

"Ariel, where are you going?"

"Oh, hey, Sheena. I forgot."

"Is your dad waiting for you or anything?"

"Nope."

Nope, she says, just as happy as usual. I can't figure this girl out.

"Come with me." I pulled her by the strap of her backpack so she couldn't get away. She just laughed at me. There were never many students inside the library after school, so we went there. I looked around, making sure no one was in ear shot. "Tell. And don't ask me what or I'll— I'll."

She waited.

"Okay, I don't know what I'll do. Just tell me how you were seeing and hearing what I saw and heard."

"You really don't know?"

"Ariel!"

"It's simple, Sheena. I'm a gleamer just like you are. Well, not just like you. We're different types."

"You know about gleamers and you know I'm gleamer? How?" I looked into her eyes. I saw it. I'd always seen it. The same shine that I saw in Mr. Tobias's eyes, that was also in Nana's eyes. The gleam.

"It's in your eyes. Just like it was in my mom's eyes. I figured no one had told you, so I waited for you to know it.

"My mom taught me. She explained it, ummm, like bedtime stories."

"Okay, girls, we're locking up."

"We're leaving," I said as I led Ariel out into the hall. "What did you mean, we are different types?" Yes, I was testing her. I knew I was the last type-one.

"Each gleamer has different gifts."

"And you've known all this time?"

"Hasn't anyone told you anything about who you are?"

"Clearly not enough."

"Gleamers glow."

"You mean my eyes?"

"Yes, your eyes, but your whole body glows because you're a type-one. Everyone can't see it, but healers can."

"But—" My mind fought with me, refusing to accept what I heard.

"Sheena, gleamers find each other. There are certain gleamers that join together. Like we are assigned to each other. We're not meant to work alone. We're stronger together."

"But Mr. Tobias, he was alone." *No, Nana... And me...*

133

"We're connected."

I can't believe this.

20

"*D*on't crowd around the doors, people. Head on out to your school bus or vehicle, guys. In the mornings, you mope around like you don't want to be here, now you don't want to leave. Let's go. If you're not a part of an afterschool program or detention, you have to go."

I didn't know if he was a parent volunteer or school security, but he was there every morning wearing a blue uniform with a two-way radio on his hip, shooing us to our classes. And then every afternoon shooing us out the door.

Ariel quickly hugged me. "You're going to be okay."

"How are you so casual about all of this?"

"Maybe because I've always known."

Chana walked slowly as if she'd been lagging back watching us. She approached, shaking her head. "Why do you act like she's the most wonderful thing in the world."

"Because she is. She reminds me of my mother. She was a type-one gleamer also."

I almost choked on air. *I know she didn't just say what I thought she said.*

"What? What have you guys been talking about?" asked Chana, just as shocked as me.

"Not only do you know that I'm a gleamer, your mom was a type-one?"

"Of course."

Of course, she says.

"Ariel, you have to come home with me."

"I don't know if I can right now."

"Then this evening. Seven o'clock." That would work better anyway. I forgot I had detention.

"My dad will be home by then. Okay."

Ariel left and Chana turned to me. "What was that? Tell me everything."

"I can't. I have detention."

"What did you do now?"

When I got home, I documented the conversation with Ariel and anything else I could think of. I had the jitters like I was hyped up on an energy drink. I couldn't believe what was happening.

Ariel was a gleamer. A healer gleamer, which I didn't know existed. Stephen Woodruff was a gleamer, but I didn't know what kind. He carried on a conversation with me within a gleam, and he knew Nana. A communication gleamer? No. That didn't sound right. The Murk was at the dance and in my class. It acted weird. Was it afraid of Ariel? I think the Murk tried to do something to Cameron. It had some plan it was working out. I needed a plan of my own. It would help to have some insight into what was going to happen. I pulled the Lumen from my drawer.

The wording was kind of weird, but ultimately told something was coming. And something about a host of angels. Not a help at all. I needed it to outright tell me what was happening, or what I needed to do to help all these kids.

The doorbell rang and one by one, my friends arrived.

"Chana, Sheena will be right down," said my mom as I ran down the stairs.

"Mama Bear," Chana replied with a hug.

"Ariel, it's so good to see you."

She hugged my mom also. "May I call you Mama Bear, too?"

"Ye—" my mom started but Chana cut her off.

"No. That's mine," she said. "You have to come up with your own."

"Don't mind her, Ariel. Come on downstairs, you guys."

"It's okay. I know she loves me." Ariel wrapped her arms around Chana, and I wanted to burst with laughter at Chana's expression.

Chana stopped walking and let out a sigh, giving in.

"I've been thinking about you guys' conversation this afternoon. What you're trying to tell us is you're a gleamer too? I don't believe it," said Chana.

"It's true." Ariel looked over at the Lumen. "What's that?"

"Just a book."

"It looks interesting. Can I see it?"

Since she was a gleamer, I pushed it toward her and waited to see what would happen. It didn't burn. Only when Teddy touched it. I still couldn't figure that part out.

Ariel spoke as she turned the pages. "Sheena, type-ones have one main directive. To fight darkness. To protect us from the Murk. That's what you were created for. Well, that's number three. One and two are the greatest commandments. But regarding the Murk, that's what you were created for and without one and two, you will never defeat them."

Ariel didn't talk like that. "How do you know that? Did your mom tell you?"

"I'm reading it right here."

"No way," said Chana, rushing to her and staring at the page. "You can read it?"

"Parts of it. There's something here about a brilliant light."

"I don't know what that is."

"And something is coming."

"Yes, I read that too."

"It's about to get really bad but…"

"But what?"

"This page won't turn. It's stuck."

"Is it?" I hadn't noticed.

Ariel stood and stepped out of the way. I tried to pull the page up.

"It looks like that's the end. Why would it end like that? There's just the back of the book."

Ariel stared at it. "No. There's a reason I can read this part. It's important we know what's back there. Here, take this," she said as she handed me her bracelet.

I pushed it back. "No. That was your mom's."

"You're going to need it."

"Why?"

"Sheena," said Chana. "Look at the page—the imprint behind the symbols—and remember what I did with the computer."

"Ariel's star." I took the bracelet from her and laid it on top of the imprint on the page.

"Whoa, look at this."

It was like a key unlocking a door. It sunk down just enough to open the page, revealing a whole other book behind the first.

The first page was written in symbols. "Where's the rest? They're all blank?"

"You want these pages blank," said Ariel.

"Let me see that." I read and looked up at Chana. "As the Murk gets stronger the pages fill. That's what it says."

"Look at the top here," said Ariel

She and I read together. Slowly, deciphering each symbol. "The hope of a child can pierce darkness."

"Why a child?"

"Adults don't believe the way we do—I mean not all adults. Life gets bad and stressful. You know how we were homeless? My dad gave up hope, but I didn't. I never did."

I nodded in understanding. Chana stood with her arms crossed, deep in thought.

We all turned, hearing feet pound down the steps. "This better be good. I have to get back home," said Teddy.

"Don't you have any manners?" asked Chana.

"Yeah, you could've said hello first," I added. At least he showed up. I didn't think he would.

"And don't talk to it anymore," Ariel was saying, still looking down at the book.

"Don't talk to what?"

"The Murk."

"You talk to them, Sheena?" asked Chana.

"It's not a them. It's one thing that divides itself."

"How do you not?" I asked Ariel.

"I just say, get thee behind me, Satan."

I laughed. "That works?"

Ariel kept glancing over at Teddy. I was surprised he hadn't commented about what he was hearing.

"It finds it funny, but eventually gives up until another time."

"I'm confused about what's going on here, but hold that thought while I go to the restroom," said Teddy.

Ariel watched him walk away and then started again. "The Murk is attracted to fear. You can't be afraid of stuff. You've talked to it. What did it tell you?"

I thought back to the day Drake and the twins came to my house. "To watch my friends."

"Have you?"

"I don't know. I guess."

"Do you want to find out?" Ariel asked.

"How?"

"Let's hide while Theodore is in the bathroom."

"How will that show us anything?" I looked at Chana, wondering what she thought.

"It sounds funny to me," she replied. "You know I won't pass up a chance to irritate Theodore. Let's do it."

We hid in the furnace room. I tried my best not to snicker as the three of us crouched next to the furnace with the door cracked open. This was going to be hilarious.

"What are you doing?" I whispered, feeling Chana elbow me.

"Getting my phone. I have to record this."

We heard the bathroom door open and Teddy walked by. "Where are you guys? They must've gone upstairs." As he walked over to the sofa, we jumped out at him.

Teddy screamed. "What are you guys trying to do?"

"Scare the devil out of you. Literally," said Ariel.

I laughed so hard I couldn't catch my breath. It was the expression on his face when he screamed and the way he jumped like he was having some kind of fit.

Ariel charged at him. "Theodore, you saved me once. Now it's your turn."

Teddy looked like he didn't know whether to stand there or do something. I ran after Ariel thinking it was part of the game. She grabbed Teddy's arm and pulled back his sleeve.

I gasped. "Teddy, what is this? What happened to you?"

"Theodore..." said Chana.

He pulled away from us. "I—" He backed away. "I need to go."

"You are not leaving." Tears filled my eyes. "What's happening to you?"

His face contorted and his eyes watered. "There's a monster under my skin."

Ariel grabbed him again, placing her hands over his scars. Teddy groaned as he tried to break free. Chana tossed her phone aside and we helped hold him. It was hard to do because he really fought to get us off. It reminded me of years ago when several nurses and my mom had to hold me down to give me a shot. They didn't expect a kid to have that much strength. He fought like that.

Ariel breathed hard as she released him and backed away.

Teddy's arm was smooth, and he looked like himself again. Ashes rose over him like burned paper flitting off to the ceiling and disappeared. Just like when the Murk left Luke Tobias.

Ariel grabbed his other arm. He didn't fight us this time.

"Stand back. Stand back," he whined.

"No, we are not letting you go—" I paused. "Wait. He's not telling us to stand back, he's singing. It's Stevie Nicks."

"It's probably the only song I know from those songs you play all the time."

"He's back."

"Whoa, she really just did that," said Chana.

"I told you."

"Are we okay? Has everyone calmed down now?"

"Sheena, you're the one who needs to calm down," said Teddy.

We all stood around Mr. Tobias' book.

"The Murk is attacking your friends, Sheena. They really want to hurt you. They were trying to get to you through Theodore."

"That's why I was cutting myself? Do you know I can't even remember doing it?"

"That's because the Murk was taking control of you."

"How?"

"You had to let it in—through anger, fear, or defiance."

"Mr. Tobias warned me about that, and I still fell right into it."

"He did?"

At that moment, I understood the warning in my dream. The Murk would keep trying to use someone close to me. "I'm trying to figure out what I'm supposed to do about what's happening. This destiny that I have, I don't know what it is."

Teddy reached for the Lumen, let out a piercing wail, and pulled his hand back. He shook his hand while we sprung toward him, trying to calm him.

As soon as he had us all hunched over his hand trying to see his injury, his yelp turned to a chuckle and he laughed hysterically. "I'm joking. It didn't burn me this time. I guess we know why."

"That wasn't funny, Teddy."

My dad didn't think so either, because he bounded down the stairs.

"Hey, Papa Bear," said Chana.

"What are you guys doing? I heard screaming as I came through the front door just now." He looked at us standing around the table with the Lumen in the center. "What is this, a seance?"

A smile formed on my face. I wanted to laugh, but he wasn't joking.

"Why did I hear screaming?"

No one spoke. We didn't know what to say or how to explain it.

"We were reading and—"

"You and this book. Give me this thing." He grabbed it off the table.

"Daddy, no!"

"You're always in this thing. It looks like some form of witchcraft. Not in my house."

"I thought you didn't believe in spooky stuff?"

"Sheena, you guys are down here screaming and standing around a book of symbols. I will not have you practicing who knows what in a Christian home. As for me and my house—"

"We will serve the Lord. I know, Daddy. That's not what that is. I need that to—"

"No, you don't."

My mom hurried down the stairs. "Jonas, what's going on?"

"He's taking my book."

"Jonas?"

My dad charged past my mom. "Is the fireplace lit?"

"Jonas!" she screamed.

21

*M*y dad stomped up the stairs, down the hall, and into the family room. We all ran behind him, yelling for him to stop. His arm went up to throw the book into the fireplace, but Ariel caught him by the wrist. My dad froze there, looking at her hand. He didn't say anything, but I had a feeling he felt something.

"Jonas!" Nana called from behind us with more authority than I'd ever heard from her or anyone else. I didn't know when she arrived but thank goodness she was there. She stepped forward with her arm outstretched. "Give me the book."

My dad lowered his arm, turned, and took it to her.

Nana placed it in her bag as my dad ran his hand over his face. "Get your father some water."

"I'll get it," my mom said, and jerked her head to the side.

I understood and took my friends to the front door. "You guys should go. I'll talk to you later."

"My dad will take us all home," said Chana while texting him.

We waited in the sunroom, but we didn't talk. After they were picked up, I went to my room.

They were all texting me half an hour later to make sure everything was okay.

I responded to each but Facetimed with Chana later that evening. Blue, pink, and green flexi-rod curlers covered her head.

"What are you doing?"

"Trying something different. I'm going to have big bouncy curls tomorrow. Maybe. If I did it right. Is everything okay?"

"I think so. Thank goodness for Nana. Anyway, I've decided I liked things better when angels and demons only existed in the Bible, and novels, and movies."

"In other words, you'd prefer to be ignorant," said Chana.

"Why are you talking to me like that?"

"Because you need to get real with yourself about what's happening and listen to the little cherubim."

"You're not usually on Ariel's side."

"I am now."

She looked behind her. "My mom is calling me. I've gotta go. Sorry to leave you to deal with this by yourself. I hope your dad's not going to ground you. Text me in a few."

I sat staring at my window. Moments later, my dad came to my room. "Nana is taking the book home with her."

I didn't look at him. "I heard."

He spoke much more calmly than I expected. "I didn't come in here to apologize. I just want to be clear about what I won't allow in this house."

I knew what he wouldn't allow. If you lived in my house, you had to be Christian. He expected me to abide by the vow of purity I'd taken. I couldn't wear red nail polish or date until I turned sixteen (the next three years were going to be interesting), and I had to go to college. Those were his rules. Oh, and I couldn't wear cropped tops that were too short, or shorts that were too short. "Everything in decency," he'd said.

"Why did a book scare you?" I asked.

"What?"

"You were scared."

"If I was afraid of anything, it was that you may be falling into or participating in something—"

"Evil."

He stood in front of me with his thumbs in the front pockets of his jeans.

"Do you think I would do that?"

"Unknowingly, kids get involved with things they don't know will cause them harm."

"So you were trying to protect me?"

"That's my job."

I looked down at the floor.

"So who screamed?"

"Teddy."

"Why?"

"He was just joking around." I thought for a moment. "We're kids, we joke and play. We've screamed before. Why were you so alarmed this time?"

My dad's head rose, but he didn't answer. He looked out my window. "That's Dingy's mom. I bet she wants you to babysit. Did she pay you last time?"

"Umm... I don't think so. Not yet."

"Well let's go and see if that's what she's here for."

Way to change the subject, Dad.

Dingy's mom needed me to babysit that weekend. So after my oatmeal and toast breakfast, and I cleaned my room, I walked over to their house.

Dingy's real name was Dinali. It was shortened to Din Din when he was a baby, then turned Dingy when he was a toddler because he was so silly.

"Dingy, when did you get a dog?" I asked when I walked in.

"He's a rescue dog. We just got him. It helps him feel safer," said his mom.

"I can relate." I couldn't tell what kind of dog he was. Maybe something with lots of hair mixed with a Labrador Retriever.

"I'm late. I'll see you guys later." She kissed Dingy, grabbed her purse and gloves, and rushed out the door.

Dingy turned to me. "Thank you, thank you, thank you for coming instead of Mrs. Beckett. She's too old anyway. I always feel safer when you're here. You're my superhero."

"Aww... thanks, Dingleberry."

"Don't call me that."

I laughed. "Why not?"

"It sounds like poop."

"You've got a point. Although I think you're obsessed with poop. Speaking of poop. We probably need to walk your dog." He kept turning around in front of the back door. "I think he's trying to tell us something. What's his name?"

"Chevy." Dingy ran to the front door. "That's the doorbell. I'll get it."

"Ask who it is before you open it!"

"Theodore! Yay! I wanted you to come. We can play."

"Hey, Dingster."

"Don't call me that."

"It sounds like poop, right, Dingy?"

"Yep."

"Oh, so you guys are teaming up on me." Teddy laughed. Sheena, do you think it's okay that I'm here?"

"As long as my dad doesn't find out. I think my almost dying on him has worn off and he's in grounding mode again. How are things at home? I mean, with your dad?"

Teddy hung his coat on a hook next to the door. "Much better. Like night and day."

"You look it."

"Let's get my racing track," Dingy told Teddy. We all climbed the stairs.

"Maybe that will keep him busy so we can discuss what we're going to do."

"What *we're* going to do?"

"You know I'm not letting you do whatever you're planning alone."

He's definitely back. He'd even gotten a haircut. I smiled to myself. I had to admit, I was glad.

"Dingy, why are there stickers all over your bedroom door?"

"To ward off evil."

"I guess the Transformers are good for something." A moment later, I heard something crash to the floor. Dingy had grabbed his toy cars, ran out into the hall, and threw them over the banister to the lower floor. His dog, Chevy, ran back with him as he grabbed more. I stood with my mouth open. "Dingy!"

Teddy stopped him. "Hey, man, I don't think you should be doing that. You're going to break them."

"I'm just trying to get them downstairs fast."

"Whoa, whoa." Teddy grabbed the racetrack from him, thinking he might throw it over the banister.

"Wait, weren't we supposed to walk my dog?" asked Dingy.

"Oh yeah," I said. "Let's do that first, just not in the direction of my house."

We walked down the street past a church.

"Let me hold the leash," said Dingy. Chevy was almost as big as him. I pulled Dingy back from going into the street and pleaded in my head for Chevy to hurry up.

Come on, dog. I know you have to go. It's starting to snow. Hurry up. Maybe I don't need a dog, but then look how cute he is.

No one else was out walking except for a man up the block. Short, dark coat, and long white hair. He turned and looked back at us. *Is that?* I picked up my pace, so I could get a closer look.

"Sheena, what's up?" Teddy looked at me and then in the direction I was walking. "Do you see something?"

The man looked back at me again. This time I waved, and he waved back. *It's him.* I didn't know how, but it was him. I jogged toward him.

"Sheena, wait."

"Mr. Tobias!" I yelled.

"Sheena, think. That couldn't possibly be him!" Teddy yelled behind me.

This man was walking. Mr. Tobias couldn't walk, but it was him.

I looked back at Teddy. He tried to run after me, but he had Dingy and the dog, who'd walked around a pole, and wrapped his leash around it with his leg caught inside.

Dingy laughed. "How did he do that?"

Mr. Tobias turned the corner.

"Mr. Tobias!" I called.

He stopped walking, as if he finally heard me, and turned. He looked so happy. And I had the biggest grin.

"Little Gleamer," he said.

It really is him. I didn't know how he was there, but if gleamers existed, anything was possible. I knew he could make things right. He would know exactly what to do about the Murk. I felt so relieved.

"You're so easy," he said as he transformed into Drake.

I sucked in my breath like it was the last I'd ever have. I wanted to run away, but I stopped moving, pressing my feet into the deicing salts on the sidewalk.

"Death can be a hard thing to accept, you know? This is good. I finally caught you away from the healer. You are more powerful together. Did you know that? It's harder to cause torment when you're on one accord."

I wanted to scream. I wanted to call out to Teddy to hurry around the corner and save me. But what could he possibly do to help? How foolish of me to run off like that. Why would I think Mr. Tobias was alive? I knew better.

Drake didn't move from where he stood, but I could hear him clearly.

"It's my world. You just live in it. Stop fighting me. As I desire, you will be."

I thought of what Ariel said. "Don't talk to it Sheena."

"We grow out of your pain and fear." The twin girls said in unison from behind him. "I, I, I, me, me, me. That opens the door. Teen selfishness. You're searching, and we find you."

I was so afraid my knees were shaking. *Don't be afraid. Ignore him, Sheena,* I told myself. *Ariel said they have no more power than you give them. Remember, if they are after you, it is because you are more powerful than you think. And like last time, you are on the brink of something. They're playing mind games. They've gotten you away from your property and away from the hedge of protection around your home.*

"Sheena!" Teddy yelled as the Murk moved closer.

"Get the-thee be-be-hind me S-Satan," I stuttered. My eyes widened. It was still there and moving faster toward me.

"I hope you're not afraid of death. Everyone has to die sometime."

I heard Dingy's dog barking before they reached me.

"We have company," said Drake.

Chevy barked and growled as they came around the corner but wouldn't walk forward any further.

"He was ours," the twins whispered.

Dingy pulled on Chevy's leash. Teddy looked ahead of us, not seeing anything, then at me. My eyes were fixed on them, like we were in some kind of standoff in an old Western movie.

Drake cocked his head to the side, waiting. That's when I remembered they couldn't read my mind and didn't know my next move until I did it. They put fear and thoughts in you and waited for you to act on them to see if it worked. The angel told me to keep my hope.

I felt something on my hand but didn't look down. It was Teddy. His gloved hand held mine. But instead of pulling me back, away from what he figured I saw, he looked straight ahead, as if he saw it too.

He spoke slowly. "Be strong and of good courage. Do not fear nor be dismayed."

I turned and looked at Teddy, taking my focus from the Murk to my friend. Determined and unafraid. The Teddy I used to know, with his nose beginning to run and snowflakes melting on his head as soon as they landed.

"Turn back, Sheena."

"Chevy, stop it. Stop barking!" Dingy yelled. "What are you two doing? Sheena, can we go home now? This dog is acting crazy. It's scared of the snow or something."

"Yes," I said, ignoring the Murk. "Let's go back."

22

"*T*eddy, that scripture you spoke—"

"Mr. Tobias said it would remind you of who you are."

"Are you ever going to tell me everything Mr. Tobias told you?"

"You'll find out as it's needed."

I punched him. "Punk."

"See that's why I don't tell you anything. But I will tell you this. You're too focused on the Murk and their power. Stop looking at who they are and look at who you are. Mr. Tobias said you're going to save us."

"He did?"

"Why do you think you're always fighting for a cause? Paper straws at school, free lunches, the clothing donation closet, and about twenty other things. It's inbred in you to fight for others." He stopped in front of Dingy's house. "Why are you looking at me like that?"

"It's just good to have my friend back."

"That doesn't sound right. That's not how you talk."

"Then how is this: You're getting on my nerves, Teddy. Get out of here. Go on home before it starts snowing harder?"

"That's a little better. You're bossier than that, though. I'll see you tomorrow."

I watched Teddy leave and went inside with Dingy.

I never had another nightmare after that day. Actually, I didn't need to dream anything. My life was scary enough.

———

There were no other signs of the Murk that weekend. And by Monday, somehow, I felt stronger.

Teila eyed me as I walked past her. "Be careful, she's off her meds."

"Oh, I'm on meds now? You have nerve—"

Chana pulled me away. "Since when do you let the FPS get to you? We laugh at them, remember? You act like you want to go around slapping everybody. That's my job, not yours."

I laughed at her. "I am not trying to get in any more trouble with Mr. Vernon."

"Right, so just walk away." Chana pointed at Teila with a mean look as she pushed me forward.

"You know I was about to jump up in the air, pause, and drop down on her."

Chana laughed so hard. "As much as I would love to see that, please don't do it."

"Really though, I just have a lot on my mind. I think it's making me irritable."

"Do you know what we need?"

"What?"

"A trip to the mall."

"After what happened last time? I don't think so."

"Remember your mom said you needed to get away from anything gleamer related for a day? You need that again. Let's go skating."

"Ice or roller?"

"You choose."

Chana and I held hands and spun around in the center of the rink. Thank goodness the music blared. It kept those around us from hearing how loud I laughed.

I wasn't as good of a skater as Chana and Teddy, but I could skate. Dancing and skating at the same time? That was a whole other skill set that I didn't spend enough time working on.

When their jam played, I always backed off the rink so Chana, Teddy, and the rest of the pros could do their thing. Sometimes I'd go over to the small rink in the next room and skate by myself. It was a good place to warm up so I could build up the nerve for the larger rink. The small rink was for little kids and beginners.

I skated forward, while Chana skated backward. "Show off!"

The DJ announced speed skate. If he didn't give that warning, skaters like me would get plowed down out there. And the pros did not like you getting in their way.

"Chana, I'm going to leave before I get trampled."

"I'm coming, too. I need a pop. It's hot in here."

"Is the whole school here tonight?" I don't know why I asked that. It wasn't like there were many places for teens to hang out in the winter in Muskegon.

Teila stood at the rail with a couple of FPS watching the skaters. As usual, they dressed alike with big earrings and matching sweats. Cameron walked up to us. "Are you guys following me? You're stalking me, right?"

We laughed. It was good to laugh. I was glad I'd come.

"Let me have a sip of your pop," said Cameron.

Chana pulled the cup away from him. "Boy, you are not putting your mouth on my straw. Do you need some money?"

"Cooties." I joked as I looked toward the rink. The center had become a dance floor, which I thought was against the rules, but they were allowing it.

Teddy rolled up to us with Justin behind him. Justin wore sneakers. I figured the rink didn't have skates to fit feet as large as his, but he said he only came to watch. "What's good to eat? I haven't been here in a long time."

"Sheena always gets—"

"Popcorn and Raisinets," Chana and Teddy said in unison.

Chana shook her head. "The only person I know who pours Raisinets over her popcorn."

"It must be the sweet against the salty, right Sheena?" asked Justin.

"Whatever it is, it works for m—" *Am I seeing things? No, I'm not.*

"Go hide somewhere," I said, looking past them. "It's here."

Cameron rolled in closer to me and looked towards the rink. "What? What does she see?"

"What is it, Sheena?" asked Teddy.

"The Murk."

"Here? Where?"

I pointed.

"That's what they look like?"

"Those are avatars."

"No way," said Cameron.

"Are you pointing at those three teens roller skating together over there? The girls are hot. Twins? Double my pleasure," said Justin, who couldn't possibly know what the Murk was.

"Nah man," said Teddy. "You don't want that. Trust me. They are not what you think they are."

"Hey cuties, roll yourself right over here," Justin called, pointing at the top of his head. "They're smiling at me."

"They've probably figured out your weakness," said Teddy.

Chana looked concerned. "Why do you think they're here?"

"This is a prime place, like a concert or a sports game. There are so many kids."

The three avatars turned toward us at the same time, in the same movement, blended into one and back into three again.

"What in tarnation?" said Justin.

Cameron squinted and scratched his head. "Tarnation? Is that like a place? Like an actual place?"

I have to do something. I skated away. Maybe the Murk would come after me and leave my friends.

"Sheena? What are you doing?" Chana yelled.

"Is she going to them?" asked Cameron.

"Go, go, go," yelled Teddy. "Follow her."

I rolled away from the concession stand, and as I did, I rolled past Teila, who leaned against the banister of the rink sneering at me. She turned to the girl next to her and whispered something.

"What do we have here?" Drake said loudly.

"Enter her," they all said at once.

"They're going after Teila!" I yelled behind me.

Teila stood upright and placed her hands on her hips. She must have thought I was about to start an argument with her. "What?"

She looked both ways. I turned and skated toward her from one direction, while Chana, Teddy, and Cameron came from the other. They surrounded her, whereas I slammed into her. I wasn't good at stopping on skates, and the red carpet outside of the rink only made it worse.

"Back! Back!" yelled Teddy. "They're still coming."

"Hey, you can't wear those skates outside," someone yelled.

"We're not!"

We stopped at the door.

"You guys are freaking me out. Is this supposed to be a joke? Payback or something?"

"Teila, something is after you because it feeds on the meanness of your heart."

"Yeah right." She pushed me. "Let me go."

"Okay, let her go, then. She's going to wish she'd listened."

"To whom? You? You don't even like me."

"Do they?" I pointed, and she looked at the three heading for us.

"Who are they?" She stepped beside me. Her voice shook. "Why is he looking at me like that—all three of them?"

"She doesn't get it, Sheena," said Cameron. "It's too late."

Drake reached his hand out toward Teila.

She gasped, and I stepped in front of her. "No, it's not."

Chana stepped in front of me with her arms out to the sides.

Drake smirked. "One way or the other, she's mine."

"No, I'm not," said Teila, almost in tears as the Murk disappeared. She screamed. "Did everybody just see that? What was that? He just disappeared."

"Trust me, you don't want to know," Teddy replied.

"I think I'm ready to go home now."

"Me too," they each said.

I sat to take off my skates. For once I didn't mind the sweaty sock smell as I put my shoes on. My thoughts were on what I'd just done. The brave version of me didn't think about what I was doing and stood in front of Teila to protect her. The same girl that would never have done the same for me. *Oh well. At least she didn't become an amber alert. But was the Murk getting desperate? The avatars showed themselves. I get it. It would ignite more fear that way and—*

"Sheena…"

Teila stood over me. I shook my head. "It's okay. You must change your heart, right now, or it won't stop coming for you. Evil attracts evil."

"I don't understand what's happening."

We left her there, watching us turn our skates in as her friends flocked around her, asking questions. I don't know if she answered any of them, but I never saw her take her eyes off me.

Happy to be safe at home, I sat at my desk, thinking. *Do the angels know what's happening here? Isn't that what they're for? To look after us, direct, and protect us?*

Then I heard voices. I walked to the stairs, and the voices stopped and then lowered. *Why are they whispering?*

"It's going to take something drastic for her to become all that she is."

There were mumbles and then, "How can we keep her here? She can't go running off everywhere. It's not safe."

The floor creaked. *Stupid stairs.*

"Sheena?"

I walked halfway down the stairs, jumped back, and screamed. "What was that? Something just ran by."

My mom laughed and walked toward the kitchen. "Why are you so jumpy? Come down here."

My dad waited near the foyer for me.

"Oh my gosh! We have a cat now?"

"Sometimes we need a little help."

"Well, your help has a gift for you," I said, watching the calico cat approach my dad with a mouse in its mouth. He held a finger to his lips and took the cat out to the front porch.

"Sheena, I made some hot chocolate," my mom called. "You want?"

"Yes, please! I can't believe we have a cat. I thought we were dog people."

"We're just animal people, I guess."

"What have you two been up to, other than adding to our family?" I wanted to know what they were talking about while I was upstairs.

My mom glanced at my dad as he walked into the kitchen. "We know you have to go to school, but other than that, at least for a while, you need to stay close to home and not go anywhere alone."

"Okay."

"Okay? That's it?"

My dad felt my forehead.

"Does she have a fever?"

"Not that I can tell."

They both studied me as I sipped my hot chocolate and scooped out a marshmallow with my spoon.

I looked up. "What?"

23

*T*he doorbell rang. A few minutes later, my phone vibrated.

Sheena, U have company and a lot of it!

Why would my mom text that? She always yelled my name up the stairs after answering the door. The only person I knew that would show up without calling was Chana. I got a little excited for company.

I walked down to the foyer, only I couldn't get to the foyer. There were so many kids, you couldn't walk through the area, and more were on the porch. "What are all of you doing here?"

"Are you not paying attention to the news?" asked Teddy over the hellos.

"Why, what happened? Did the school burn down?"

"Are you paying attention to the amber alerts on your phone?"

"No."

"Okay, get out of your bubble," said Cameron. "Kids are disappearing again."

"I know."

"No, you don't. I mean, like crazy. Look at your phone, Woman."

I pulled it from my pocket. There were forty-five alerts I hadn't checked.

"Today a white—"

"Van...."

"You *do* know?"

I couldn't tell them about my dream.

"What are we going to do? Is there a plan?" asked Corey.

Through the entrance to the living room I watched my mom. She stood listening with her arms crossed in front of her. "Mom, this is Nelson Middle School's eighth graders. Nelson Middle School this is my mom."

They exchanged hello's and I whispered to Teddy, "I'll be right back. Take them all downstairs, please." I hurried up the stairs and stood leaning against the hall wall. *What is happening? There are bookworms, FPS, Sporties, and Jokers in my house. Do they know my secret? Who told them? And they expect me to know what to do about whatever is happening.*

I went down the hall to the bathroom and splashed water on my face. The girl staring back at me in the mirror frowned with water dripping from her face onto her shirt. What was I supposed to do?

"Sheena, what's going on?" My mom asked from the door.

"I have no idea. I think they want to discuss what we can do as a school because so many kids are disappearing."

"So they chose our house for a meeting?"

I shrugged. "We have a big basement."

"Why didn't they call first?" she asked while turning away. I could still hear her as she walked down the hall. "I hope they're not expecting snacks. I think I have a bag of M&M's. They'll be lucky to get two apiece."

When I got to the basement, my classmates were all talking at the same time, engrossed in several conversations. There was hardly room to walk.

A kid burped loudly. *Justin is here too? When did he get here?* His body seemed to take up most of the room.

"I'm trying to understand undertones," Bradly was saying. "Like this lipstick is a blue red, but then there's an orange red. I mean, they're all red—"

"And your mom is going to smack you if she catches you wearing it. Sheena, put on some real music. You're killing my ears."

"Would you please stop staring at me like I took a poop on your lawn?"

"But at some point, you say, what is meringue anyway?" Justin was saying. "I mean, it's not whipped cream, or is it?" The kids around him laughed.

"What are you talking about? Stop with the meringue stuff. It's egg whites and sugar, okay?" I said.

They continued laughing and turned toward me as I walked through the group. "Get off the pool table, please."

"Sheena, educate them on what's happening," said Ariel while standing.

"Why?"

"It's the only way many will be saved."

"She sounds like a prophet or something," said one of the unmentionables.

"Sheena, is it true what we've been told?" asked a kid who'd just been trying to get someone, anyone, to pay him to do a handstand. "We thought you were different. We didn't know you were crazy too."

Chana stood. "Shut it. Don't make me—"

"Okay, okay. Listen closely because I will never repeat this. If you bring it up, I'll act like I have no idea what you're saying.

"You guys know me—well some of you. And if you do, you know I don't care what you call me, or say about me. I have no reason to lie about anything."

I lifted my backpack from my shoulder and removed the Lumen from it. Only Nana and I knew she hadn't taken it with her.

"The Murk has existed from the beginning of time."

"That's the dark force from Stephen Woodruff's books," one of the bookworms said with eyes wide. "I knew it was real."

"You're right. It *is* real, and it's getting stronger." I placed the Lumen on the table. Everyone stood around it and watched me open it to the back blank pages. They gasped as writing appeared. "As it strengthens, the pages fill."

"I'm getting out of here," someone said.

Cameron's cousin, Corey, blocked off the hall. "Anyone who tries to leave will meet my fist."

"Well, that's one way to handle it," someone replied.

"You can leave, but I think you should hear her out," said Teila. She nodded at me to continue.

"Hey, what's that last part, the writing or symbols look different. The color is goldish too."

I hadn't noticed it before. "Help is coming."

"What does the rest say?"

I looked at Chana and she nodded. "It's telling the future of mankind if the Murk isn't conquered."

"Like what?"

"I can't say."

"Endgame, I think," said Cameron. He surveyed those in the room. "So are you in or not?"

"In how?"

"We need an army."

"Who told you that?" I asked.

"I just know."

"How can we be an army?" asked Justin.

Corey looked at him like he meant business, as if we were there to start a revolution. "You need to believe."

"Have hope," said Chana.

"Be prayed up."

Ariel nodded. "Get rid of fear."

"Or stay in the safety of your ignorant world and forget everything you've heard," Chana added.

"Anyone that tries to leave will meet my—"

Chana grabbed his shoulder. "We know, we know. Thanks, Corey. Sheesh."

A girl with sandy-brown hair raised her hand.

"We're not at school," someone said with a laugh.

"Relax, let her speak."

"How do you know all of this and that we can actually do this?"

I looked around at my friends. "We've done it before."

"Who?"

Cameron, Chana, Teddy, Corey, and lastly, Bradly, stepped alongside me.

"Bradly, really? You too?" asked Teila.

"Yes. We were a team. We did it together. I can tell you firsthand, this is real. You can't be afraid. And if you don't join us, the guilt will mess you up."

"Sheena, do you have powers? Like, would you be able to save us if something goes wrong?" asked one of the jokers, more serious than I had ever seen him.

I shook my head. "I just know things. I'm not like a superhero or anything."

I took a deep breath. I appreciated them. All of them. But I couldn't let them help. Not when I knew this was some kind of grand stand. "You guys mean well, and I appreciate you, but you can't help me."

"Don't start that again, Sheena," said Teddy.

"I won't put you in danger."

"It's dangerous?"

I stepped closer to her, the bookworm. "Very. It's been described as *The Hunger Games*, only worse."

The room fell silent for several seconds. I think what I was trying to tell them finally sunk in.

"Go home, guys. Be safe. And keep me in your prayers."

"Are you sure, Sheena?" asked Ariel.

"Yes."

"May your future be forever in your favor," said one of the sporties.

"That's not how it goes."

24

I stopped Ariel before she left.

"We all came together, Sheena, so I need to hurry before they leave me."

"Okay, just one question."

She waited.

"The Murk seems almost afraid of you. I haven't been able to figure it out. I don't think It can affect your mind at all either."

"It can't. That doesn't stop it from trying. But I'm not like everyone else. Haven't you noticed I'm a little different?"

I wanted to shout, "Are you kidding me? Of course, I have. Who hasn't?"

"The Murk doesn't understand how my mind works."

"Why?"

"Autism Spectrum Disorder."

"You're autistic?"

"Mildly, or higher functioning, they call it."

"No you're not."

"I'm serious."

"But I've studied it. I know the type of things that should bother you, but it hasn't."

"I think that's because I'm a gleamer. It wasn't that way when I was younger, though. I couldn't talk before. Can you believe it? That's why I'm in eighth grade instead of nineth. Bye, Sheena. See you tomorrow."

This time I watched her walk off like she always does, in the middle of our conversation, like she didn't have a care in the world, and I was glad she was my friend. That little chat explained so much.

I expected lots of weird looks the next day at school, but if I'd bet on it, I would've lost. I couldn't believe the kids that came to my house didn't spread a rumor around.

During lunch period, Principal Vernon, on his daily stroll through the cafeteria, glanced over at my table. He stopped walking for a minute, looked at me with a raised brow, and motioned toward the kids around the table. I shrugged, and he continued on.

I wasn't surprised when I was called down to his office during the next period. He did his principal pose where he sits back in his chair with his legs crossed at the knee, his elbow on the arms of his chair, and his hand propped on his chin with his pointer finger under his nose.

"Have a seat, Sheena."

"Am I in trouble? I haven't gotten into any fights, I've gone to detention, and Teila and I are friends now."

He pointed to me. "That's it. That's my point right there."

What point? You haven't even said anything yet. "I don't think I understand, sir."

"In the cafeteria, who sat next to you today?"

"Chana."

"On the other side?"

"Teila."

"She's never sat at your table before, has she?"

He asked a question, but he didn't stop talking to let me answer.

"Neither have the fifteen other kids. You guys even pulled up another table to make room. So I asked myself, 'What's going on? Why is Sheena's group of friends so popular all of a sudden?' Don't get me wrong, I'm happy to see you guys getting along, but I also notice patterns."

"What kind of patterns?"

"Patterns that tell me something is going on. When you guys got into it with Cameron a few weeks back, the next thing I knew, you were suddenly friends. Then he shows up

175

after I follow you and Theodore to the apartment complex of someone that had been abducting children and helps subdue the people involved. He wasn't just there. That was planned. So..." he said as he leaned forward and clasped his hands on his desk. "What's happening now?"

Great. Why did I ever use the gleam on him? "I haven't planned anything, if that's what you're thinking."

Principal Vernon settled back in his chair, I think a little relieved.

"We've just noticed that kids are disappearing again."

"Yes, I'm aware of that. So what you're saying is, you haven't any idea who's doing it this time because you didn't mention that part?"

I studied Principal Vernon and he studied me. How was I supposed to tell him about the Murk? How do you explain that? I didn't even want to, but I could tell he knew something.

He reached for a book on his credenza. "Is this real?" He pushed the opened book toward me and pointed at a section of a page that described the Murk.

25

"Close your mouth," my mom would've said if she saw me. I read the section of the page Principal Vernon pointed to and looked up at him.

"How did you know about this?"

"I paid a visit to someone we've both encountered."

Nana? No, I don't think so. Stephen Woodruff? He could've talked to him at school. But he said encountered, not met.

He waited for me to figure it out, but I didn't. "Luke."

"Luke Tobias? You went to the prison?"

Principal Vernon nodded while removing the book. We'd reached for it at the same time. My hand lightly brushed across his and pulled back. "I'm trying to get my head around this. Knowing what you can do makes me believe it, I think. This thing it mentions—it's out there?"

I nodded.

"Sheena, I stand behind my words. If you need anything from me, or if anything is going on, you let me know. Do not go out there on your own again. If anything develops, let me know."

From the look he gave me, I almost said, "Yes, dad." I guess I had another interim father.

<hr />

"Sheena, where have you been?" asked Chana as she fell in step with me, looping her arm through mine. "I've been looking all over for you."

"Principal Vernon's office."

"Again? Why?"

"You won't believe it."

"Yes, I will, walk this way." We hurried down the hall toward her class.

"He asked me about the Murk."

"He knows?"

"Yes, and he has Stephen Woodruff's book. And get this, he went to the prison to see Luke Tobias."

"Nooo…"

"Yes."

"What did he find out?"

"Luke Tobias couldn't remember a lot of stuff, but he confirmed the dark force that Stephen Woodruff wrote about. Like, it pretty much freaked him out and he had to be carried out."

"Mr. Vernon told you all of that?"

"No, I touched his hand by accident and saw it. It only took seconds.

"The Murk leaves everyone crazed and helpless like that after they get what they want from them."

I walked into Chana's class, still talking, and sat at the desk next to hers.

"What's he going to do with the information?"

"I don't know."

"Wow."

"I know, right?"

There was one more thing Luke Tobias told Principal Vernon that he didn't share with me. I guess he wouldn't have told me, and I didn't want to tell Chana. I could still see and hear Luke clearly in my head. "That girl—that girl who was there. The one that was in my head..." He looked around and then whispered, "She's in danger. It's gonna get her." He nodded as if responding to a question while looking up to the left with a blank expression.

"Sheena!"

"Yes?" I sat up in my seat and faced Mrs. Chisholm.

"Did you miss me?"

"Huh?"

"I just figured you must've missed me because you already had my class earlier today, and you're back."

"Oh, yeah. Mrs. Chisholm, I think I need to go over everything again. It wasn't really clear this morning."

The class watched in amusement. Everyone was crazy about Mrs. Chisholm, but she was no joke. She wore hoop earrings, her hair was cut in a really short tapered afro and she dressed like—well, like normal people. T-shirts, sweatshirts, and jeans instead of teacher wear—flowered shirts, and stuff.

"Is that so?" she asked.

I nodded. "Definitely so."

"Okay. You may stay."

"I can?"

"Sure... If you can answer a question for me."

I looked at Chana, and she shrugged.

"Don't look at your buddy. Are you down?"

"Uh, okay, I'm uh, down."

"Good. When is an atom stable?"

I strummed my fingers over the desk. "When it explodes?"

The class burst with laughter, and Mrs. Chisholm pointed at the door. "Better luck next time. I'll expect the answer to that tomorrow," she yelled after me.

Chana ran up to my locker after school. "Boo!" she said from the other side of the door.

"I think it's going to take a lot more than that to scare me after what I've been through."

"Yeah, you're right. So listen. I want you to come with me. No questions asked."

I looked at her skeptically. "What are you planning under that curly bun?"

"Sledding."

"Where?"

"Behind the school on the hill back there. Everyone's going."

"Okay, let me text my mom. Since it's here at the school and there will be lots of people there, she'll probably say it's okay."

I ended up having to beg and told her Chana's dad would bring me home.

There were so many kids out there after school, the hill looked like a kaleidoscope of color from all the coats. It wasn't too steep of a hill, but it was enough for a fun time. Most of the kids lived nearby and had gone home for their sleds. When you lived in a city that could have snow from October through May, it was a good idea to own a sled.

Others, like me and Chana who didn't go home, had to share. Some had makeshift sleds, some had wood ones, others had plastic. Cameron slid on his stomach on what had been a huge cardboard box. Chana and I raced, with me sliding down the hill on someone's yoga mat. I flipped over and ended up covered in snow. I sat up, brushing the snow from my face, and was raring to go again.

I pulled out my phone to go live, showing all the kids sledding. That was one of my mom's conditions. She had to see how many people were actually there.

"Hey, guys. Check it out," I said as I zoomed in on the sledders. "Watch, watch, watch!" I yelled. Cameron tried to run and dive onto someone's sled. It was a fail. "Ooh! He's such a goofball." The pain showed on his face as he flipped over.

"Are you recording?"

"I'm live!" I laughed.

It never failed. When you're having fun, something always happens. A few feet from us, a girl flew down the hill and crashed into someone. Everyone ran to her. I'd seen injuries from sledding before. They weren't pretty. "Gotta go. Let me make sure she's okay," I said and shut down the live feed.

I heard my name called. Teddy walked near the back of the property, waving. He flipped over onto the snow, making fun of the face dive I just had, and waved for me to come to the area he was in. I looked back toward the girl. Chana had run over to her.

"Bring her to me," I heard and looked around to see who had spoken.

I took a step in Chana's direction to point out that Teddy was there. Suddenly my body hit the ground and I felt myself being pulled back. Before I knew it, I was flying across the snow field on my back at an incredible speed.

Not one person noticed. I tried to cry out, but my throat filled with the chilling air and caught there. Then I noticed the wind blowing over, causing the snow to cover my tracks. I was dragged back into the wooded area beyond the field, between the school and the highway. I stopped abruptly and backed up against a tree, catching my breath and frantically looking around. Laughter came from the kids on the hill behind me and sounds of traffic from the roadway beyond the trees.

"Sheena Meyer, I presume. Yes, it's you," he laughed at himself.

Drake formed and walked toward me. His approach reminded me of that of a cat. Maybe a panther. Panthers stalk their prey and then rush and spring several feet at them for the kill.

There was no one around to help me, and I wasn't sure how I was supposed to fight it. I pushed my back against the tree as if I could dissolve through it, and its bark could protect me.

Before Drake could get close, globs of snow dropped from the tree branches above me. My arms flew up over my head to shield me from the large clumps.

Chana landed on the ground in front of me with her arms outstretched.

"Stay back. It's time you gave up," she said. "Move on or whatever you have to do. But leave her. How many times have you tried to take us down? That old vendetta has to give. After the big fire in Chicago, you moved here. You tried to destroy this city with the fires of 1874, 1891, then again in 1946. It is always the same. You build your army and then try to destroy everything by conflagration. We're still here. Haven't you learned by now that you cannot win?"

Conflagration? What is she talking about?

"Thank you for that, but I know the history of this city as well as you. The time of the gleamer is over."

"That may be true, but not until you're over. Gleamers exist because of you. If they're over, you're over."

"There is nothing you can do to defeat me."

"But *she* can."

Drake and the twins ran forward, and I braced for whatever was coming. But then a bright beam of light shot out from Chana. I couldn't believe my eyes.

"You are forgetting the rules of the guardians," came a voice that wasn't hers. I mean, I hadn't heard her sound like that. Like an adult goddess or something.

The light blinded me, but in an instant was gone, and so was the Murk.

Chana stooped beside me. "Are you okay, She-she?"

"Is it dead?"

"No."

"So for the last time, who are you again?"

26

O ver the next few days, I went to school and straight home afterward. I didn't ask to go anywhere, not even to Chana's house.

"Are you being fearful?" asked Chana, over the phone.

"No, just careful."

The Murk was showing up more, and more of my friends were getting involved. I could feel what was coming.

"Sheena!" my dad called.

"Gotta go."

"I didn't do it," I yelled playfully as I headed for the stairs.

"No one has heard from Nana, and she didn't show up to her community center meeting. We're going over there."

"What?" My eyes were wide, and I got teary, thinking the worst.

My dad put his arms around me. "Calm down. We don't know anything yet. She could be fine. We're just going to double check."

"But the police can do that thing where they go and check on people."

My dad turned to my mom. "She's right."

"That's *my* mother. I need to see for myself. Let's just go," she said as she handed me my coat.

We pulled onto Nana's street, a long road with few houses and lots of land. Only a thirty to forty-five-minute drive from our house, we called it the country. "Nana lives in the country," is what everyone said if asked, as if she lived somewhere down south.

The front of Nana's house looked as peaceful as always with a pretty wreath on the front door. She had one for every season and every holiday. We walked up the three steps and rang the doorbell. No one responded. I rang it again.

"Why is it echoing like that?"

"Mom, use your key."

She unlocked the door and slowly pushed it open. I bumped into her because she stopped in her tracks and didn't go any further in. I looked around my mom. The back of the house had been plowed through. It was gone.

It broke my heart to see Nana's home destroyed. My mom held her stomach as she looked around in shock. "What happened here?" Her voice was tiny like a child's.

My dad rushed in front of us. "Someone's in here!" A body lay on the floor. His leg moved.

"Who is that?"

I recognized his clothing. "He's an author. Stephen Woodruff."

My dad lifted the drywall debris and turned him over.

Blood streaked over his face. Mr. Woodruff had trouble speaking. He curled his fingers, motioning for my dad to come closer. "It took her," he whispered.

"What took her?" asked my dad.

"Nooooo!" I yelled. "Where? Where is she?"

Mr. Woodruff's eyes stared ahead. I thought he'd died, but his head turned to me. "Come closer," he whispered. I knelt beside him and lowered my head. His hand shook as he reached for me. He touched my forehead. "The sun is there. Capture it."

"I-I don't know what that means."

"You've seen it," he tried to yell. "See with your heart, Sheena. Fight with your heart."

"What is he talking about?" asked my mom.

"I don't know."

I shook, feeling a vibration within me. "We need to get out of here."

"I agree. The house may not be stable." My dad carried Mr. Woodruff onto the front lawn, and an ambulance came. Then he received a call from Chana's dad. "We have her," he said. "She's at Hackley hospital. Tell Belinda she's going to be fine."

Relief swept over me, and I hugged my mom tight as she cried.

On the way to the hospital, my mom bombarded me with questions. I had to explain how I knew Stephen Woodruff and that I didn't know Nana knew him. She'd thought it was something like her not knowing about Mr. Tobias and was relieved to find he was just an author that visited the school.

At the hospital, we rushed in, but had to wait for someone to take us back to Nana.

Restless and tired of going back and forth between sitting and pacing in front of my mom, I decided to go over to the snack machines.

"I'm going over to the vending machines. Do you want anything?"

My dad sat with his arm around my mom and motioned for me to go ahead. My mom shook her head. She looked as if she were about to break down. I didn't know what to do to help her. After Chana's dad said Nana was going to be fine, I had to believe she was okay. I just wanted them to hurry up allow and us to see her.

"Let's see. Peanut butter crackers? Nope. Pretzels? Nope. Granola Bar? Nope. Trail mix? That'll do." I placed a dollar in the vending machine. It glided back out, I placed it inside again, and it slid right back out of the slot. "Daddy, I'm going to need another dollar," I said over my shoulder. "This is a perfectly crisp dollar bill," I mumbled to myself. "This machine is discriminating against my dollar. There are no wrinkles in it. What? It's not the right shade of green or something?"

A zip of light passed over me and off to my right, up near the ceiling.

Oh my gosh! Is that—? Oh my gosh! My angel is back!

My heart leaped within my chest. I wanted to cry, I was so overjoyed and relieved. I was in such need of help and answers.

"Where are you going?" I heard my mom ask behind me.

"There are more machines around the corner," I yelled.

I followed it down the hall and around a corner. It stopped near a stair exit as if it had just noticed me. I smiled, waiting for it to transfigure.

"I know you've been here healing people—I guess in the ER this time, but I am so glad to see you. I missed you— If that's okay to say." I didn't get too close. I didn't know if it would like that.

It began to transfigure into a being of light. I grinned watching it and looked behind me to make sure no one was coming down the hall. When I turned back, a dark smoke swirled from the ceiling down to the floor. Drake and the twin girls stepped out of it.

"It's been many years since a gleamer such as you was born. But you are covered in fear. It reeks from you. We watched your mother, but it wasn't her."

"You've been watching my family?"

"Watching and waiting for generations. You have an annoying ability to resist. Not anymore. Where you've been weak, the Murk has grown stronger.

"You said you missed me? Let's see how much." Drake extended his hand and I began to pull toward him. I grunted and squirmed, trying with all my might to scream and pull back. My hand reached for the wall and tried to hold on, breaking a nail as I dug at it.

"Open up. Let me see where your strength lies."

My eyes watered. I couldn't speak. I wanted to tell my parents and Nana I loved them. I wanted to thank Chana and Theodore for being my friends. I wanted to tell Ariel how special she was. But there would be no time. I weakened and felt something within my body slipping away. At that moment I realized the Murk used Nana to get me away from Chana, Ariel, and the hedge of protection around my home. I knew I'd go to heaven. At least, I thought I would. But I wasn't ready to die. *I'm sorry I failed.* I whispered within me.

27

I was losing the battle. Not just for me, but for all the gleamers and for all kids. I could feel Drake pulling at me. Not just my body, bringing it toward him, but at what made me me. He was trying to take it from me, and I held on as long as I could, drifting and sinking away into that feeling I felt in my nightmares.

Something rumbled behind me. Double doors swung open. Hands wrapped around me and snatched me out of the Murk's grip. It shrieked with anger as I was swept around the corner and down the next hall. I think I blacked out for a moment. I saw a scene, an image of my ancestors and the land. Eyota and her family. They migrated to Michigan. To Muskegon. Nana's house was built on their land. Generations of gleamers came from that land. It's blessed. The last gleamer would come from that bloodline.

I lay crumpled on the floor, taking deep breaths, like I'd been without oxygen for a while and needed to feed on it. "An oxygen vampire," I said aloud.

Nurse Javan laughed. "You always say the funniest things every time I see you."

I looked up at his grey scrubs and into his eyes. The glow was there. "You saved me. Why?"

"So you can save others."

My eyes watered. "But I couldn't save Nana. How can I save anyone?"

"Everything is not what it seems. You are the answer and the question."

"Where is the sun I need to capture?"

"In you. The Murk must fall."

"Then make it fall. Why can't you do it?"

"It is your destiny, Little Gleamer. The gleamer destiny. The key is the sun."

My mind flashed to images of Ariel's bracelet and the dream I had. I got as close as I could get to the sun, reached my hand out, and touched it. I felt a surge of energy.

"The forces that are for you are greater than the forces against you. Remember that."

I blinked and looked around at the empty hospital corridor and slowly sat up.

The sun is within me. I've already captured it. I have to figure out how to use it.

Nana rested in our guest bedroom. I stared at the tv, its volume low. Amber alerts were scrolling across the bottom of the screen. Disappearances from all over the tristate area.

I slowly closed the bedroom door, quietly so it wouldn't wake her. *I'll handle this, Nana. The Murk will never hurt you again.*

I knew where the stand would take place. On our land. Nana's land.

Mr. Woodruff was in the hospital but doing well. He wasn't hurt as badly as we'd thought. He had looked much worse.

"Is he talking?" asked Teddy.

"I don't know."

"Let's call the hospital," said Chana. We were on a three-way call. "I'll do it. My voice sounds more adult than you guys. Plus, you guys don't know how to merge the calls."

"Knock yourself out," said Teddy.

We waited. "They're putting me through," she said, her voice filled with excitement and surprise.

"I know, we heard."

"When he picks up, you talk, Sheena."

"I know that, Teddy."

"Okay, I just wanted to make sure you weren't quiet and waiting for us to talk."

"Hello?"

"Mr. Woodruff?"

"I was expecting your call."

"I figured."

"Ask your question."

"Why did it come after Nana—Valerie?"

"To get to you." That's exactly what I thought.

"But her hedge of protection—"

"It can't cross that, but it can use a human to do what it needs."

"Why am I not given instruction like to speak to the wind or anything?"

"You have been given the ultimate instruction."

"To capture the sun?"

"Remember that different things may be required in different seasons. But if you capture the sun, you have everything you need."

"What will happen if the Murk isn't destroyed?"

"The way they feel, do you know that feeling?"

"Yes." I pictured how I felt at the hospital and in my dream with that eerie darkness creeping over me. The sludge. "Darkness. Fear. Pain. Sorrow."

"Yeah, I've had that feeling inside of me. It's horrible," said Teddy.

"Teddy!"

"Oops!"

"Sheesh!" said Chana.

"It's okay. I knew you were on the call. That feeling will spread like a viral pandemic."

"How?"

"You've seen kids who seem to hate everybody and everything?"

"Yes They're really dark and act like they don't care about anything."

"The Murk already has them. It will take over their minds. All good will be lost. All compassion. All that will remain is despair. And despair demolishes faith."

"Why kids?"

"To start a faithless generation."

I thanked Mr. Woodruff and ended the call.

"Well, that's all we needed to know. The Murk has to be stopped or the world as we know it is over for our children and children's children."

"Theodore, stop being so dramatic. Sheesh," said Chana.

"I'm not. I'm just stating facts."

"You guys, stop it. I'm going to let you go, I need to think," I told them.

"Alright, double trouble. Text me with the plan."

"Bye, Teddy."

"Bye, big head," said Chana.

I waited. "Chana?"

"You know I'm still here."

"I'm going to see if I can spend the night at your house tonight."

"And I'm going to figure out a way to get us there."

"Where?"

"Wherever you're planning for us to go."

28

We crawled into Chana's parents' bedroom and to the side of their bed. As her dad snored over us, his arm fell over the side, almost smacking me in the head and giving me a heart attack. We both froze for a moment.

Burp!

"Really? Could you burp a little louder next time?" Chana whispered.

"Sorry, it was an accident." Some burps can't be controlled. She shouldn't have given me all of that pop.

Chana reached on the nightstand for her mom's phone. We must have kicked up some dust because I was about to sneeze. I covered my nose. She looked at me as if to say you better not.

I crawled backward as fast as I could and ran down the hall just in time to sneeze in Chana's room. Chana quickly tapped over her mom's phone, pulled up an app for a car service, and typed in our pick-up address.

"Your mom has a credit card attached to that app. Won't she see the charge?

"I'll deal with it when the time comes. I mean, we are about to save the world. That should account for something. Let's just make it through the next few hours so I can live to be grounded for life—again.

"Where are we going?"

I thought of Drake. I'd heard him in my head a few hour before. "Come and come alone."

"Let me do it." I typed in the address. "Okay, there's a car seven minutes away. I'm going to add a note for it not to beep its horn upon arrival."

"They don't do that, do they? I thought they just messaged they'd arrived."

"Oh, okay."

"Let's get something warm to drink."

I sat, nervously trying to figure out how I would get out of Chana's house alone. *I could drug her hot chocolate, but that would be wrong and where would I even get sleeping pills? I've seen too many movies.*

"What's wrong?" asked Chana.

"Nothing. Just thinking." I looked at the phone. It showed a map of the neighborhood with the car just around the corner. I sat up.

"What is it, Sheena? Do you hear the car?"

"No." I faced the pantry door and walked toward it. "I hear something in there."

Chana grabbed a cast iron skillet. "Are you sure? That door sticks. Maybe something's trapped."

I nodded.

She slowly opened the door and peeked inside with the skillet raised at her shoulder. Whatever it was was going to get clobbered. As she pushed the door further, I walked up behind her. Chana went all the way inside the pantry and looked around the shelves of food. Over her shoulder she asked, "What did you hear?"

I closed the door behind her. Sure enough, it stuck.

"Sheena? Sheena, listen to me. I know what you're trying to do."

"I love you, Chana. We're not just best friends, we're sisters—always will be," I said and ran to the side door.

"Sheena! No! Let me out!"

I ran out of the house and jumped into the backseat of the car. "Quick, go!"

"Uh, excuse me, little girl. Who are you trying to run from? Are you running away from home?"

"No."

"Where is your parent? I am not about to lose my job over this. They are not going to have me on the news talking about I took a child somewhere. Do you understand? I can't take you anywhere without someone eighteen or older. Are they coming out?" He looked out of the passenger side window toward the house.

I looked down at my lap. I had nothing—nothing I could come up with to make him leave. What was I going to do? *Please, please, please. I need help.*

A moment later, the guy put the car in reverse and backed out of the driveway. "Do you guys have enough heat back there?"

"Yes," I said. A tear dropped from my eye. Someone helped. I looked behind me out the rear window as Chana ran out into the street. Her arms flew up and back down hard at her sides.

<hr />

The driver didn't say a word. He hummed to music all the way to Nana's property and stopped in front of the house. "You guys be safe," he said as I got out of the car.

You guys?

I stepped up onto the sidewalk and watched as he made a U-turn and sped away. I almost didn't want him to leave—well, leave me there alone. But I'd thought this out, right? It was the only way to keep everyone else safe. The Murk told me to come alone.

My boots crunched through the hard snow as I walked around Nana's house and into the field behind it. The land resembled a huge white lake, still, with no signs that even animals crossed it. Beyond the field were sparse trees and

then another field. I kept going. My breaths formed small clouds in front of me as I trudged on, not knowing where

to stop. I'd never been aware of where Nana's property ended and the next one began.

"I'm here! Everyone else can live now, right? You have what you want." I yelled.

I turned, looking around. The night was totally silent. I had no light other than what came from the full moon and bounced off the snow.

"I'm here," I yelled again.

Drake appeared about a couple hundred feet away. "It touches my heart how you'd give yourself for them. If I had a heart. Which I do not."

"Stop hiding behind your avatars. What are you really?"

"Do you want to see what I am?"

Did I? The thought of it suddenly terrified me so much that I didn't know if I was shivering from the cold or fright.

Drake extended his arms out to the sides as if he wanted a huge hug. He disappeared and what replaced him rose sixty feet into the sky. Dark and threatening, worse than any image I'd seen of it thus far. A black swarm of muck and smoke. The sludge. Ruled by hell.

I stumbled back onto the ground. What had I done? Why was I there?

"To save them, all you have to do is open your heart to me. It won't hurt. Release it until it is empty and let me fill it."

I'm the key. If I release my hope, it takes over.

Images flashed through my mind. My Nana, friends, and family dying.

"No!" I yelled as I grasped the sides of my head. "Stop!"

"Then you will serve me?"

29

I lay crumpled in the snow. My heart beat fast. I didn't know what was coming. How would the Murk take me? Would it hurt? I heard my dad's words in my head from when we first got our cat. "Sometimes we need a little help."

That's when I heard something and looked behind me.

"Aye!" yelled the group of people running toward me screaming. "There she is! We're here, Sheena! Hold on!"

There were a good sixty of my classmates running toward me. Lights swung back and forth from flashlights.

"Chana told us where to find you," Cameron said as he ran up and knelt beside me.

"How did you guys get here?"

"The See You at the Pole kids, my dad's church busses and Principal Vernon." He stood with them. Cameron's father and Chana's parents were there also.

"What do you need us to do?" asked Principal Vernon.

"I don't understand. Who organized this?"

Ariel stepped forward with her father behind her.

Principal Vernon looked all around. "Are you sure something's out here?"

"Oh, it's here, alright," said Ariel.

"Where are they? It?" yelled Cameron. They all held some form of weapon: Bats, brooms, golf clubs, BB guns, Bibles.

A hot blast of air shot toward us. We covered our faces.

"What was that?"

"A better question is, what *is* that?"

I squinted, trying to see. We all fell silent. Something was moving toward us on the ground.

"Oh my gosh. Look how many there are," said Bradly.

The Murk's horde of kids marched forward and stood below it. The number of them was staggering.

"The twins are over there. Charles and Charmayne. Remember the two that were rescued?"

"This is what we've trained for," said one of the See You at the Pole kids to those beside her. I guess that meant they were spiritually ready—prayed up. I hoped that prayer had prepared them to handle what they might see.

"Let's get'em," said Corey.

"No, they're all brainwashed and under the Murk's control. They don't know what they're doing."

"The kid in the black shirt. Is that Theodore?" asked Principal Vernon.

"Oh, no."

"How is he over there?"

"You know that passage in the book of Luke, right?" asked Cameron. I kept forgetting he was the son of a minister. Half the time he didn't act like it.

Cameron continued. "It talks about when an unclean spirit comes out of a man, how it says it will return to the house it left and on it's return finds the house all clean and in order. Then it goes and brings seven other spirits more wicked than itself, and they go in and dwell there."

"And the final plight of that man is worse than the first," his dad added.

"I'm gonna—"

"No, you're not gonna do anything, Corey. I came here alone because the Murk said it wouldn't hurt any of you if I came. All of you would be safe. That's the same thing it told Theodore. That I would be safe. It just fills your head with lies."

"What are we going to do? Leave him there?"

"Let them go," someone yelled.

The Murk's horde stood like statues.

"What are they waiting for?"

One of them wasn't waiting. Theodore took steps toward us as if he was having to drag his legs to do what he wanted them to do.

"Wha-what is he doing?"

"Theodore, stop," Principal Vernon yelled with his hand outstretched.

Teddy didn't take his eyes off me. He just kept coming.

"It's controlling him."

He got close enough for me to see the struggle on his face. He was trying to fight—inside him.

Three of the boys from the unmentionables group stepped forward. "He needs to remember what's real."

One of them ran, and the other two followed.

"Boys, no!" yelled Principal Vernon.

They each grabbed Teddy, but he successfully threw them off. As he walked, they kept trying to hold him and stop him. Then I saw why they were pulling at him. Teddy held a knife.

I jumped up and ran to Teddy. Ariel followed, screaming my name.

"Teddy!" I yelled.

He stopped and watched me.

"I know you won't hurt me no matter what it does to you. I know, Teddy. I know."

"You don't know anything," the Murk replied as Teddy thrust his blade forward.

30

I tried to keep everyone out of it. Somehow, my friends were there anyway. Maybe that's the way it was supposed to end.

I heard Chana scream my name, but it was too late.

The blade went right through my coat.

Chana continued screaming, and then she was beside me. "No, no, no, no! What did you do?"

Teddy still held the handle of the blade, and suddenly awoke from the trance of the Murk. "What-what happened?" He let go of the blade and stepped back. "Nooooooo!" he yelled as he crumpled to his knees.

I looked down at the knife sticking out of me and pulled it out. There was no blood. I unzipped my coat and let it fall to the ground so I could remove the bag beneath it that held the Lumen. *It saved me.*

A horrible sound came from the Murk. "It's angry. Come on."

"You're okay?"

"Yes, go."

Ariel grabbed Teddy's arm and Principal Vernon pulled him to standing. We all backed up toward the others, hearing the roaring from the Murk.

It began to swell and expand. "Something's happening."

The horde beneath it began advancing again.

"Drop your weapons. Hold hands."

"What?"

"Just do it. Close your eyes." I prayed. "They need to know why we fight. Let them see. Please allow them to see."

"Open your eyes," I told them.

They all stepped back, seeing the dark image of the Murk rise to the sky over the kids. Some gasped. Someone screamed.

"What in tarnation?" said Justin.

"Whatever you do, do not lose hope. That thing is not stronger than our hope. If you have to leave, leave, but do not lose faith here," said Chana.

I grabbed Teddy. "We know that wasn't you. We don't need your shame right now. We need your faith."

"Ariel, did you do the thing to him?" asked Chana.

"Yes, it has released him."

"Wait, what?" asked Principal Vernon, looking at Ariel as if seeing her for the first time.

"Good job, honey," said her dad.

I stopped talking. *I'm coming,* I heard in my head.

"My angel?"

Your earthly angel.

Ariel stepped to my right side, Chana at my left. Cameron and his father, his cousin Corey, Justin, Teddy, Principal Vernon, and Bradly behind them. Everyone else lined behind and alongside them.

"Did those kids not just see what happened with Theodore?"

"They can't see anything."

"Don't do this! You don't know what you're doing," Cameron yelled at the kids approaching us. "My people are destroyed for lack of knowledge."

"They need to know what's controlling them. They have to be shown."

"How?"

The kids ran toward us. "Hold your place!" I didn't know what was going to happen, but it was going to happen whether I wanted it to or not. I trembled inside, but I had to be strong for those around me. They trusted me. *Is this truly my fate? This is where my destiny was supposed to bring me? To my death?*

We all looked down, feeling vibrations in the ground.

The kids stopped just short of us. We backed up and closed in toward each other, looking around.

Marching came from behind us, the sound of hundreds of feet.

"Are they surrounding us?" asked one of my classmates.

"That's a military move," said Corey.

Principal Vernon shielded me with his body. "You guys stay behind me."

"Look!" said someone from the back of our group.

The crowd parted. I turned to see what the Murk was bringing in to attack us with next.

I stared at the man walking in front, leading a multitude of people. "Daddy!" I screamed. "How are you here?"

I ran to him. As I did, a sword of energy shot out from the Murk. My dad ran forward, pushed me to the side, waved his arm, and it disintegrated. I looked up at him in shock.

Corey covered his mouth and his legs stomped quickly from his excitement. He and Cameron slapped hands. "Yeah! It's about to get real!"

Behind my dad was Nana, Stephen Woodruff, my mom, and Mr. Tobias's son—the doctor. And many others.

"Who are these people?" I don't know why I asked that. All of their eyes glowed, including my dad's.

The gleam.

I looked up at him, not understanding.

"It takes two gleamer bloodlines to produce a type-one gleamer."

"You're a gleamer? You mean you believed the whole time?"

He didn't respond. His focus was on what the Murk and its horde were doing behind me.

"Can you make it stop?"

"This is spiritual warfare, Sheena. You prayed for help. We've brought it."

I looked up over my dad. The guardian angel of each of the gleamers stood with them. *They* couldn't see them, but I could. My mouth dropped. Glowing figures, fifteen feet tall or more, stood together.

Energy began to expand out from the gleamers as their angels charged at the Murk, fighting on our behalf.

I was filled with so much awe and appreciation and— love. I don't think I ever felt more hope or faith in my life. I was so full, literally.

That's when it happened. The angelic beings stopped and looked back at me, all of them. I opened my heart.

"No!" cried the Murk.

"Please open their eyes. If just for a moment. Allow them to all see what I see."

Most of the adults dropped to their knees at the sight of the angels and the Murk. Some of the students also. The horde of kids came back to themselves. Some screamed, others looked bewildered.

An energy shot out of me that normally no one would've been able to see but me. I didn't feel pain, just peace and love. I hadn't captured the sun, but *the* Son. That was the mystery.

There was an explosion of light in front of us as the Murk yelled out. Sparks as if from fireworks and ash floated down all around us, staining the snow.

All was silent for a long moment.

"Did we do it? Is it over?" asked Bradly, hugging Teila at her side.

I collapsed and heard in my head as I drifted away, *Because you believed. It was your faith, hope, and love combined with the power of those that you helped believe, that you helped have hope. They made you stronger.*

"Are you my angel?"

"I am the archangel, but I speak for someone greater."

31

I opened my eyes. My classmates were kneeling or standing all around me. Everyone looked so scared.

"It's really cold out here."

"Get her coat."

My mom helped me up. One by one, they hugged me.

"You did it!"

"No. We did it. All of us. Remember this day. The day the city of Muskegon came together and defeated evil."

"How are we supposed to get all these people home?" someone asked.

"I'm sure we'll figure something out," said Principal Vernon.

Everyone helped the kids that had been under the Murk's control. I gave up my coat to one of them. She was crying and out there in her pajamas.

"Where did you come from?" I asked.

"Lansing."

"How did you get here."

"I don't know.

"It's going to be okay," I told her. "It's over."

"But I don't even know where I am," she cried.

I looked past her. "Mom, can you help her," I called behind me.

She walked up quickly and put her arm around the girl.

I left them and ran toward the figure I saw crossing the field.

"Hey! Chana!"

She stopped walking and turned back as I approached her. "I'm really proud of you, She-She."

"That's great, but where are you going?"

She smiled. "You don't need me anymore."

"What are you talking about? I'll always need you."

"My job was to protect you. I was a living expression of His love for you."

"My life is not over. I'm going to need a lot more protection. Do you not know the kind of shenanigans I'm capable of?" I attempted to joke.

"It's not up to me, but know I've enjoyed this assignment more than any other. Thank you for loving me," she said as she backed away.

My eyes teared. "Chana…"

She kept walking.

"Please don't go."

She didn't stop and she didn't look back.

"Chana!" I screamed. I watched her until she disappeared beyond the trees. I looked for her parents. They were gone too.

What was I supposed to do without my best friend?

<hr />

"What would you like for breakfast, Baby Girl?"

"Don't you already know?" I joked. "What kind of gleamer are you, anyway?" I stared into my dad's eyes. There it was. The gleam. I guess he no longer needed to hide the shine.

"Wouldn't you like to know?"

"Yes, I would. This family has too many secrets, O deflector of fiery darts of the enemy," I laughed.

"Well, one day we'll sit down and discuss it all."

"You'll have to make an appointment with my assistant because I have a busy schedule."

"Ha!" My dad sat a plate of pancakes in front of me that he'd already made. I ate quickly, hoping the food would calm the aching in my stomach, as I pushed back thoughts of Chana. I'd already cried in the shower, realizing I wouldn't see her at school.

My dad threw a frozen grape at me. "Is your lunch ready?"

"I thought I'd buy lunch today."

"You?"

"Yes, me."

"What about the extra lunch you take for anyone that doesn't have lunch?"

"What, I can't buy them lunch?"

"You better not be buying lunch for a boy," he called behind me.

"Who me?" I responded innocently and laughed.

Before I left for school, I walked into the family room and hugged Nana over the back of the couch. "Why are you always up so early, Nana?"

"I'm just on a different schedule than you are, sweetie," she said as she glanced over at Checkers, our cat, resting on the window seat.

"Nana, why don't you like cats?"

"They're sneaky. Look at how he's looking at me."

I laughed. "He didn't even do anything. Don't worry. Checkers will grow on you."

"Hmph," came from Nana.

I went back to the kitchen. "Just wait until he brings her a mouse," my dad laughed. I hugged his neck hard.

"Hey, what's all this?"

I backed away an grabbed my backpack. "I'm just happy you're my Daddy."

I didn't stick around for a response. It wasn't necessary.

My mom met me at the front door. "Ready for school?"

"You mean I'm actually going to get there on time today?"

"Just get your coat. The car is already warming up."

"So, Mom, what if we saw a—"

"Sheena, don't start with the crazy. It's too early."

We talked and laughed all the way to the school. Everything outside looked better. The snow looked brighter. The trees, void of leaves, and covered in ice, were beautiful. We weren't even bothered by the slow movement of the student drop-off line.

My mom pulled me to her and kissed my head before I got out of the car. I playfully pulled away from her. "Everyone can see, Woman."

"Oh, see, now your dad has you calling me 'Woman?'"

"I'm playing, Mommy."

"I know."

"Have a good day."

My hood covered my head, so maybe no one noticed me as I walked into the school. There was no whispering. Just kids clamoring around, trying to hurry and get to class.

I sat in homeroom and stared at Chana's chair. A few kids smiled at me. I didn't think those separate groups in the lunchroom would ever be the same again. And I was happy that things were going to get shaken up a bit.

As my homeroom teacher took attendance, Ariel walked in and hugged my neck before sitting in front of me. That girl was going to make me a gusher one day.

Another girl walked in and sat at Chana's desk. I smiled at her and turned away. I looked out the window, trying to hide the tears that were welling up. I had to talk them back down. *It's okay, Sheena. It's okay. You're going to be okay. Just keep her in your heart, and never forget her.*

I watched a bird fly past the window and used my shoulder to wipe away a tear that rolled down my cheek.

"You're in my seat," I heard someone say.

I spun around.

I think I jumped from my desk. We landed on the desk beside hers.

"Sheena, are you trying to kill me?" Chana laughed.

Ariel giggled while helping me up.

"Ladies, please take your seats."

We sat at our desks. Chana looked straight ahead.

"If you don't stop staring at me, I'm going to punch you."

I was so full of joy I could've turned somersaults up and down each aisle of the room.

"How are you here?" I whispered.

"Someone really loves you. You must've captured the heart of the Son."

Please Leave A Review

Your review means the world to me. I greatly appreciate any kind words. Even one or two sentences go a long way. The number of reviews a book receives greatly improves how well it does on Amazon. Even a short review would be wonderful. Thank you in advance.

Review here:

https://www.amazon.com/dp/B08684WD8B

Don't miss out!

Exclusive content, discounts and giveaways are available only to L. B. Anne's VIP members. Use the link below to sign up. There's no charge or obligation.

https://www.lbanne.com/vip-club

ABOUT THE AUTHOR

L. B. Anne is best known for her Lolo and Winkle book series in which she tells humorous stories of middle-school siblings, Lolo and Winkle, based on her youth, growing up in Queens, New York. She lives on the Gulf Coast of Florida with her husband and is a full-time author and speaker. When she's not inventing new obstacles for her diverse characters to overcome, you can find her reading, playing bass guitar, running on the beach, or downing a mocha iced coffee at a local cafe while dreaming of being your favorite author.

Visit L. B. at www.lbanne.com

Facebook: facebook.com/authorlbanne

Instagram: Instagram.com/authorlbanne

Twitter: twitter.com/authorlbanne

Made in the USA
Monee, IL
24 March 2021

63695597R00135